D0835749

# EINSTEIN the PENGUIN

**Iona Rangeley**

Illustrated by David Tazzyman

HarperCollins *Children's Books*

First published in Great Britain by
HarperCollins *Children's Books* in 2021
HarperCollins *Children's Books* is a division of HarperCollins*Publishers* Ltd
1 London Bridge Street
London SE1 9GF

www.harpercollins.co.uk

HarperCollins*Publishers*
1st Floor, Watermarque Building, Ringsend Road
Dublin 4, Ireland

1



ISBN 978-0-00-847596-3

Iona Rangeley and David Tazzyman assert the moral right to be identified as the author
and illustrator of the work respectively.
A CIP catalogue record for this title is available from the British Library.

Typeset in Arno Pro Regular 13pt/24pt
Printed and bound in the UK using 100% renewable electricity at CPI Group (UK) Ltd

This book is produced from independently certified FSC™ paper
to ensure responsible forest management.

For more information visit: www.harpercollins.co.uk/green

*To my parents, even though they never let me have my own penguin*

## Chapter One

# London Zoo

It was a very long time ago now, as long ago as last Christmas, that the Stewarts first met Einstein.

It was a cold sort of Christmas. The sort where days end early and forget to start on time, and the fairy lights out in the street don't quite make up for the darkness.

'What can we do with the children?' said Mrs Stewart to her husband one Saturday towards the beginning of December. The early afternoon was bitterly chilly, and no one had found the heart to venture out into it yet. 'We don't want them to get too bored. Imogen might paint the cat again.'

Mr Stewart sighed into his tea and turned a page of his newspaper. 'She's grown out of that sort of thing, hasn't she?'

'I don't know,' said Mrs Stewart. 'Maybe.'

The children, at that precise moment in time, were keeping themselves busy in the sitting room. Arthur, who was six, was drawing pictures in a notebook while Imogen, his big sister, was sitting cross-legged in the corner, fiddling with the dials on a radio. Occasionally it would make a crackling sound and then stop again, and she would triumphantly declare to her brother that she had 'fixed it'.

'Maybe we should take them to the zoo!' said Mrs Stewart suddenly.

'The zoo?' Mr Stewart repeated.

'Yes!' said Mrs Stewart, who had spotted an advertisement on the back of her husband's newspaper.

'Arthur might like to draw the animals!'

Mr Stewart frowned into the article he was reading. He rather liked the idea of going to the zoo. It was exciting: maybe he'd see a lion! 'Well, all right,' he said eventually, in a careful sort of voice. 'If you think the children will enjoy it.'

'Imogen! Arthur!' Mrs Stewart called, and Imogen came skidding into the kitchen on the slippery tiles. Her brother followed calmly a few moments later. 'Get your shoes and coats on. We're going to the zoo.'

'The zoo?' said Arthur.

'Yes. As a treat. It's very cold outside, so wrap up warm. Imogen, where's your jumper? You haven't lost it again, have you?'

Several minutes of rushing about the house passed. Imogen's jumper was retrieved from the cat, and three separate arguments were had about scarves. By the time they stepped outside and made their way

towards the bus stop, the sky had gone through a whole new shade of grey, and the sun – no doubt a little bored of waiting – had hidden itself behind the tall trees on the edge of Hampstead Heath.

'It's cold,' said Imogen, reluctantly taking her father's hand as they crossed the road.

'I *did* tell you to put a scarf on, darling,' said Mrs Stewart, who was just a bit ahead of them.

'My scarf is *pink*!' said Imogen. 'I don't *like* pink any more!'

'She's nine, you know, Rachel,' said Mr Stewart through a smile. 'Very grown-up.'

The bus was a Saturday afternoon sort of busy, bustling with shopping bags and umbrellas. There weren't enough seats for everyone, so Arthur sat on his mother's lap while Imogen stood up in the aisle, swinging happily on the handrail each time the bus jolted to a stop.

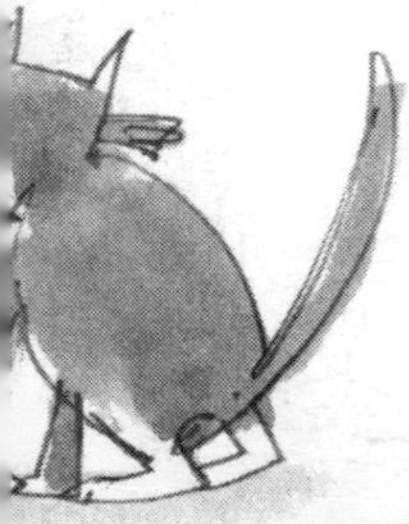

When they got off, the sky was greyer still, and there were leaves blowing in the cold wind as they walked alongside the canal.

There is something about chilly afternoons that makes people all the more determined to enjoy themselves, and the Stewarts weren't the only family in London who had thought the zoo might be a sensible place to spend their teatime: it was very busy.

The children were immediately anxious to examine all the sweets in the gift-shop window, while Mr Stewart – having had a brief panic about whether he'd lost his wallet – found it and went to buy tickets.

'Right, where to first?' he said, returning a moment later with a map.

Imogen declared that she wanted to see a polar bear, and make friends with it.

'I don't think they have polar bears,' said Mrs Stewart, taking the map from her husband. 'Why don't we wander past the monkeys and finish up at the penguins?'

Imogen pursed her lips and frowned, but the idea of monkeys was a good one, and she quickly cheered up. After a few moments, *both* of her parents were having to shout at her to slow down.

'Where does *that* monkey come from?' said Arthur, clutching his father's arm at the sight of a particularly large gorilla. Imogen was a few metres ahead, frowning at it with her face pressed to the wall of the enclosure.

'Africa,' said Mr Stewart. 'But most of them were born at the zoo. Look here – can you read the sign?'

'This one's my favourite,' said Imogen, wrinkling her nose and blowing air into her cheeks in an effort to look like the gorilla. 'Can we take him home?'

'You'll have to ask the zookeeper very nicely,' Mrs Stewart said. 'But shall we have a look at the flamingos first?'

Imogen started to shake her head, and explain that

she would much rather see the wolverines because their name sounded made up, when Mr Stewart barked that everyone should follow *him*, and marched off in the general direction of the lions.

'Why are we going this way?' asked Mrs Stewart. 'Imogen wants to see the flamingos.'

'The *wolverines*!' Imogen corrected. She was staring down at the map, which she had stolen from her mother's handbag, and without looking where she was going trod on the back of Arthur's shoe.

'Well, Arthur wants to see the lions,' said Mr Stewart firmly.

'I'd rather have an ice cream,' said Arthur, glaring at his sister and pulling his shoe back on to his foot. It was the sight of an ice-cream stand that had caused him to stop so suddenly.

'Why do you want an ice cream?' said Imogen. 'It's freezing.'

'Well, perhaps the flamingos would make a good

compromise,' Mrs Stewart suggested.

'That's not a compromise – that's just doing what you want to do,' said Mr Stewart.

'You're only saying that because you want to see the lions!'

Eventually they decided that, provided they were quick, they would have time for everything, but Mr Stewart spent so long looking at the lions, and Imogen spent so long looking at the wolverines, that they ended up with no time left for the flamingos at all.

'Well, that's it!' said Mrs Stewart, in her cross-but-pretending-to-be-polite voice. 'We'll have to go home – the zoo's about to close!'

'But we haven't seen the penguins!' cried Arthur. 'You said we'd see them last!'

'We can have a quick look on our way out,' said Mrs Stewart reluctantly. 'We have to go past them anyway.'

The penguins were outside, with their own beach and a great big pool of water that they were happily diving in and out of. Imogen watched them excitedly and cheered whenever one made a particularly big splash, while Arthur sat a short distance away from her, drawing a picture in his notebook.

'Imogen, look,' said Arthur suddenly. One of the smallest penguins had walked right up to the glass, and was peering at him.

'Oh, he wants to be our friend!' said Imogen, rushing to join her brother.

'*My* friend,' Arthur corrected.

'Don't be mean,' said Imogen. 'He can be my friend too.'

The penguin tapped its beak against the glass, and looked from Imogen to Arthur and back again.

'Look!' cried Imogen. 'He likes us!'

When they walked along the edge of the enclosure,

the little penguin waddled beside them, as if it knew exactly what they were thinking, and when they stopped, it stopped too, and squawked and shook its wings.

'I think he's the best penguin here,' said Arthur.

The penguin squawked again, and looked pleased with itself.

'Imogen! Arthur! There you are!' Mrs Stewart appeared suddenly through the crowd. 'What *have* you been doing? It's time to go home.'

'We've made friends with a penguin!' said Imogen. 'Can we keep him? Please?'

Both children were crouching close to the glass, staring at the penguin longingly.

'Please?' said Arthur.

'Come on,' said Mrs Stewart, reaching out a hand for Arthur to hold. 'We can't stay any longer or we'll be late for supper.'

Arthur looked reluctant, so Mrs Stewart gently rolled her eyes and crouched down to face the penguin. 'And *you*, Mr Penguin, must come and stay with us whenever you like. Penguins are always very welcome at our house.'

The penguin looked up at her blankly, and ruffled its feathers.

'There, will that do?' said Mrs Stewart to Imogen and Arthur. 'Can we head home now?'

'All right,' grumbled Arthur, and they followed their mother out towards the gift shop.

## Chapter Two

# A Penguin Comes to Stay

Back home, the Stewarts settled into one of the early evenings that December tends to demand. The sky had fallen asleep with even more enthusiasm than it had done the day before, and no one was left with any choice but to eat crumpets with butter by the fireside, and wait for supper to finish cooking.

Mr and Mrs Stewart sat on the sofa, watching the news, while the children crouched by the coffee table, squabbling over a jigsaw puzzle.

'Keep your voice down, Arthur,' said Mr Stewart. 'I can't hear the telly.'

'Imogen's hidden a piece of puzzle,' said Arthur sulkily.

'I have not!' said Imogen. 'Arthur hid it!'

Mr Stewart sighed and went to check on the lasagne. 'It looks like it might snow soon,' he said when he came back.

'Really?' said Imogen. 'How can you tell?'

The windows of the living room were foggy with condensation, and Imogen rushed over to wipe one clean with the back of her hand, and stare into the darkness. Outside it was foggy, and the Christmas lights of the corner shop opposite gave the misty air a tinge of yellow. She couldn't see any snow, but it did look cold – as much as outside *can* look cold when one is busy being warm by the fire.

'I think there's someone by the lamp post,' said Imogen suddenly.

'They're probably just walking past,' Mrs Stewart said.

'No,' said Imogen. 'They've stopped.' Then, after a moment, she added, 'They're very small.'

'Well, come away from the window,' said Mr Stewart. 'I'm sure no one wants you staring at them.'

Imogen went to help her brother with the puzzle again. Then, about a minute later, the doorbell rang.

'Supper's nearly ready!' Mr Stewart grumbled. 'Who goes ringing around at this time?' He stood up reluctantly from the sofa, and went to answer the door.

'Erm, Rachel . . .' Mr Stewart's voice sounded nervously from the hallway a few moments later.

'Yes, dear?' Mrs Stewart called.

'I was just wondering, Rachel, why there's a penguin at the door.'

'A *penguin*?' said Mrs Stewart.

The children looked up from their jigsaw, looked

at each other and then raced into the hallway. Their mother quickly followed.

It was true: there was a penguin at the door.

In fact, it was the very same penguin the children had seen at the zoo just a few hours earlier. And now it was waiting on the doorstep, with a small blue rucksack and a patient expression on its face.

'You haven't accidentally ordered anything online, have you?' Mr Stewart asked.

'What – a penguin?' said Mrs Stewart.

'Well, there was that mix-up last week with the teabags—'

'Yes, James, but a *penguin*?'

Mr Stewart frowned. 'No,' he said. 'I suppose that *would* be rather difficult, wouldn't it?'

The penguin looked at them blankly.

Arthur coughed, and tapped his mother on the arm. 'You did say, Mummy, that he could come to stay whenever he liked.'

Mrs Stewart looked alarmed. 'Why, yes, I suppose I *did* say that – but I didn't really mean . . .'

'You should never say things you don't mean!' Imogen piped up.

Mr and Mrs Stewart looked at each other.

'What are we going to do?' asked Mrs Stewart.

'Well, I suppose –' said Mr Stewart slowly – 'I suppose, given that he's knocked on the door, that we ought to invite him in for supper.'

'Yes,' Mrs Stewart nodded. 'That makes a lot of sense.'

'Can we keep him?' cried Imogen.

'We'll take him back to the zoo in the morning,' Mrs

Stewart corrected. 'He's obviously lost.' She turned to the penguin, and looked down at it kindly. 'Well then, Mr Penguin, I suppose you'd better come in and have something to eat.'

But the penguin had already waddled into the hall. Mr Stewart shut the door behind it, and politely took its bag.

'Do penguins like lasagne?' Arthur wondered aloud as they all went through to the kitchen.

It turned out that this penguin liked lasagne a lot. Its table manners, however, left much to be desired. The penguin, who sat at the head of the table, had finished

almost all of its lasagne before anyone else had started eating, splattered half of it on to the floor, and never once bothered with a knife and fork.

Meanwhile Gizmo, the cat, took one look at it and shot upstairs to the bathroom to hide in the laundry basket.

'Gosh,' said Mrs Stewart through a nervous laugh. 'Don't they feed you well at the zoo?'

The penguin blinked at her.

Suddenly Imogen pulled her chair close to the table and tried to eat *her* lasagne without a knife and fork too.

'Imogen!' said Mrs Stewart. 'Stop that!'

'You didn't tell the penguin off,' Imogen retorted.

'The penguin is a *guest*,' said Mrs Stewart. 'And you are *not* a large flightless seabird. Is that clear?'

'Yes, Mum,' said Imogen sulkily, and sat properly again. 'What does it say on his bag, Dad?'

The rucksack was quite old and ragged-looking. At the top, dangling from a strap, was something that looked like a name label.

Mr Stewart put his glasses on and leaned across the table. 'It says Einstein,' he said.

'Einstein?' said Arthur.

'Yes,' said Mr Stewart. 'I suppose that must be what he's called.'

'Well, Einstein,' said Mrs Stewart kindly, 'I hope you enjoyed your supper.'

Einstein looked at her gratefully and shook the feathers on his neck.

'I wonder what's in his bag,' said Imogen.

Mrs Stewart was halfway through a sentence that

sounded an awful lot like, 'It's very rude to look through other people's things,' when Imogen jumped up and undid the zip, tipping the rucksack over as she did so. It burst open.

'Oh, gosh!' said Mrs Stewart through another nervous laugh, as several silver fish flopped out on to the dining-room table. 'I suppose that's what penguins eat, isn't it?'

'You certainly came prepared, didn't you?' said Mr Stewart heartily. 'We'd better keep these in the fridge.' He scooped the fish into a bowl and rushed away with them.

'Now,' said Mrs Stewart a few moments later, after the excitement of the fish had died down, 'we should work out where you're going to sleep, Einstein. Children – clear the table, please.'

Imogen and Arthur had never cleared the table so quickly. They had probably never cleared the table so badly, either – but everyone was far too preoccupied with the presence of a penguin to take much notice.

Mr Stewart fetched Arthur's old baby blankets from the airing cupboard, while Mrs Stewart pointed Einstein to the armchair by the fire. He seemed very happy with his own chair to sleep on, and belly-flopped straight on to the cushion while Imogen draped one of the blankets over his back.

'Can we read the bedtime story downstairs with

Einstein?' asked Arthur, and Mrs Stewart looked just about ready to agree when Imogen pointed out that Einstein was already fast asleep, and everyone tiptoed up the stairs to bed.

## Chapter Three

# Sunday Breakfast

Einstein was still asleep when Mrs Stewart crept down the stairs to make coffee early next morning. He was breathing deeply from his chair near the fireplace, so that the air that rushed through his beak sounded like something between a snore and a foghorn, and made Mrs Stewart jump.

'Gosh,' she said to herself shakily, and turned on the television in order to listen to the news.

After that, Mrs Stewart went to boil the kettle in the kitchen, and opened the fridge to reach for the milk.

On this particular morning, however, the milk had been pushed a few centimetres back from its normal place, and Mrs Stewart found herself clutching a small handful of silver fish.

She jumped back, screeching, in response to which Einstein woke up, squawking, and Mr Stewart came barrelling down the stairs, ready to swat something with his newspaper.

'Ah, yes,' said Mr Stewart, pausing when he spotted Einstein, and huffing and puffing several times. 'Penguin,' he said helpfully. 'Just a penguin.'

'I *know*, James,' said Mrs Stewart. 'Why is the fridge full of fish?'

'Well, I had to put them somewhere,' said Mr Stewart defensively. 'And they'd start to smell pretty quickly in the cupboard, you know.'

Mrs Stewart rolled her eyes and carried on making the coffee.

'What's going on?' Imogen's voice piped up, and

her parents turned to see her walking down the stairs in her dressing gown, rubbing her eyes sleepily.

'Oh, nothing,' said her father. 'Just a penguin. We're about to call the zoo.'

Imogen stopped, and her face darkened. 'No, Dad, you can't!'

'What do you mean?' said Mr Stewart, picking up his phone. 'Don't you want him to go home?'

'But he's happy here!' said Imogen.

Everyone turned to the sofa, where Einstein was cheerily belly-flopping after a passing bluebottle.

'Won't he be happier at home, with his penguin parents?'

'What if he ran away on purpose?' said Imogen. 'Maybe they're mean to him at the zoo, and don't give him any lasagne!'

Mr Stewart started to dial the number from the phone book. Imogen watched him, glowered, opened and closed her mouth several times, and then stormed back up the stairs in a whirlwind of pyjamas and slippers.

'Ah, hello,' said Mr Stewart, in his businesslike telephone voice. 'London Zoo? James Stewart speaking. Yes. No. Not a ticket enquiry. No, wait – Look here. We seem to have got hold of one of your penguins.'

There was a long pause.

'Hello?' Mr Stewart continued. 'Yes, of course, do fetch your manager. Yes— Hello? Hi. One of your penguins, yes. We think it must have followed us home from our visit yesterday. Stayed the night, seems happy enough, but perhaps you could send someone to collect it?'

There was another pause.

'Rachel!' said Mr Stewart, aghast. 'They hung up on me!'

'Well, it is a very strange request,' said Mrs Stewart, handing him his coffee. 'Maybe it would help if you explained everything a bit more, and didn't talk so matter-of-factly. Here, let *me* have a go.'

Mrs Stewart took the phone from her husband, and dialled the same number.

'Hello? Now, look, I know this must sound very silly, and the truth is we're just as confused as you are, but the penguin we spoke to at your zoo yesterday has shown up on our doorstep, and as you can imagine we're at a bit of a loss.'

She paused to listen, and took a sip of coffee. 'No? Oh – hang on. But there *is* a penguin here. I—' She pulled the phone away from her ear. 'James, they hung up on me too!'

'Ha!' said Mr Stewart.

'James, this is *not* a competition!'

'Oh, yes,' said Mr Stewart bashfully. 'I suppose not, dear. Sorry.'

'They said they aren't missing any penguins, and that if we prank-call them again they'll report us to the police.'

'Ah,' said Mr Stewart gravely. 'I see.'

Mr and Mrs Stewart sat down at the kitchen table and looked troubled.

'Suppose we *did* keep him?' said Mr Stewart, after a very long pause.

'Don't be ridiculous,' Mrs Stewart snapped.

'No, no, of course not, dear – you're quite right.'

They both turned to the armchair where Einstein, bored at last of the bluebottle, had started to watch the news. The presenter, a short man with a big nose, was talking about the weather in Australia. Einstein squawked vaguely, in a way that suggested he was listening.

'He does fit in rather well, though, doesn't he?' said Mr Stewart.

Mrs Stewart took a thoughtful sip of coffee. 'Yes,' she said eventually. 'He certainly seems to, but he must be so lonely! Imagine how you'd feel, dear, if you were forced to live among a colony of penguins.'

Mr Stewart's eyes glazed over, as if he was considering the idea, and wasn't entirely opposed to it.

Suddenly a thunder of feet came rattling down the stairs, and Imogen and Arthur rushed into the kitchen.

'You *can't* send him back to the zoo!' said Imogen.

'We've googled it!' said Arthur.

'Animals shouldn't be kept in captivity,' said Imogen, though she stumbled over the last word slightly because it was very long and she was much too cross to remember it properly. 'They should be free to go wherever they want. And Einstein wants to stay here – and it's his right to be allowed to!'

'How do you *know* he wants to stay here, darling?' Mrs Stewart asked.

Einstein squawked from over by the telly.

'*See,*' said Imogen. 'That squawk means "I want to stay here and live with you forever".'

Einstein gave another smaller squawk, and went on watching the news.

Mrs Stewart sighed resignedly. 'Well, the zoo doesn't seem to want him, so I'm afraid he might *have* to stay with us until we work out what to do with him.'

Imogen and Arthur grinned at each other.

'What are those labels on his bag anyway?' Mrs Stewart asked.

Mr Stewart put his reading glasses on and pulled the rucksack over. 'They look like flight labels,' he said.

'Flight labels?' said Mrs Stewart. 'From where?'

Einstein looked up, hopped down from the armchair and waddled over to join them all at the kitchen table.

'This one says Sydney to London.' Mr Stewart frowned. 'How odd – it's only from last week.'

'What have you been doing in Australia, Einstein?' said Imogen.

Einstein stared up at them and tilted his head to one side.

'Maybe he's an Australian penguin,' said Arthur.

'There aren't any penguins in Australia,' said Imogen knowingly. 'It's too hot.'

'There are *some* penguins in Australia,' Mr Stewart corrected. 'On the beaches.'

'But penguins live in Antarctica!'

'Well, he *might* be from Antarctica, but he might be from Australia.'

Einstein gave an excited hoot, and everyone turned to look at him.

'Interesting,' said Mr Stewart, and then repeated himself. 'Antarctica?' he said.

Einstein looked blank.

'Australia?'

Einstein hooted again, and bounced slightly on his little webbed feet.

'He can understand what we're saying,' said Mr Stewart in amazement.

'I knew he did!' said Arthur excitedly. 'You do understand us, don't you?'

Einstein gave Arthur a look as if to suggest that he did.

'What else is in his bag?' said Imogen. 'There might be more clues.' She started to grab hold of it, but stopped herself. 'If you don't mind us looking, of course,' she added politely.

Einstein shrugged his flippers, as if to suggest that he didn't.

Mr Stewart had a look. Now that all the fish were gone, they could see that Einstein had brought several other things with him too – all a little slimy with fish scales. Several photographs were scattered across the

bottom, and a small Polaroid camera sat in the corner, wrapped in a handkerchief.

Einstein squawked loudly from the floor and flapped his flippers impatiently.

Mr Stewart looked a little frightened. 'Oh, dear. What does he want now?' he whispered.

'He just wants to get on the table so he can see,' Arthur explained. He picked Einstein up and placed him on top of one of Mrs Stewart's cookbooks.

Einstein waddled across the table towards his bag. He stuck his head inside and started to pick the photographs up, one by one, and place them down on the table. The first was of Einstein in Australia, outside the Sydney Opera House.

The second was Einstein at an airport, and another showed him arriving in London. The next few were selfies: outside Buckingham Palace and the Houses of Parliament, and hiding in a handbag in the back of a taxi. The most recent one showed Einstein at the zoo.

'Oh . . .' said Mrs Stewart slowly, as if something very important was occurring to her. 'So Einstein isn't from London Zoo after all?'

Einstein gave a resigned squawk, to thank her for finally realising.

'Well, that explains why they didn't take our calls,' said Mrs Stewart. 'But, Einstein, how on *earth* did you get inside the zoo and back out again, without anyone noticing?'

'He's very little,' Imogen pointed out. 'He can probably squeeze into tight spaces.'

Einstein gave a sort of nod – as much of a nod as a very little penguin is able to give – and stepped in and out of Mrs Stewart's handbag by way of demonstration.

Mrs Stewart looked impressed. 'They call you Einstein for a reason, I suppose.'

'What do we do then, Mummy?' said Arthur. 'Can we keep him?'

'Well, I don't know,' said Mrs Stewart. 'I suppose, if he'd *like* to stay with us – and it doesn't seem like he has anywhere to go . . .'

'So we're a hotel for holidaying Australian penguins now?' Mr Stewart scoffed.

'Oh, come on, James,' said Mrs Stewart. 'You were the one who wanted to keep him a minute ago.'

Mr Stewart grumbled his assent: he didn't really mean his scoffs and mutters, but thought that, between himself and Mrs Stewart, one of them always needed to be acting sensibly, even if they both got distracted and had to take it in turns.

'But only until we work out where he comes from,' he said. 'I don't suppose we can pack him off to Australia if he doesn't have a home to go to . . .'

'Well, Einstein,' said Mrs Stewart, 'you've a place to stay with us for as long as you need one. Penguins are always very welcome at our house.'

## Chapter Four

# Einstein Goes to School

Imogen got ready more quickly than usual on Monday morning, and came downstairs just in time for breakfast – though she was still brushing her teeth, and appeared to be missing a sock. Mrs Stewart, who was a teacher at the big school, was frantically looking for the homework she'd been marking, while Mr Stewart shook crumbs out of the toaster, and wondered how busy work would be at the hospital.

'Where's your brother?' asked Mr Stewart, as

Imogen yawned and dropped toothpaste down her skirt.

'Dunno,' said Imogen. She spat into the sink and sat down at the table.

'What was that?' asked Mrs Stewart. '*Dunno?*'

Imogen, as a matter of fact, did know: her brother was still in bed. He had fallen asleep with Gizmo the cat on one side of his pillow, and Einstein on the other. Neither creature had seemed particularly pleased with this arrangement, but neither had been willing to give up their turf, and all in all the conflict had made all three of them far too tired to get up when Arthur's alarm clock rang.

'Arthur!' Mr Stewart shouted up the stairs. 'Breakfast! School!'

There were several loud stomping noises, and Arthur appeared in the kitchen two minutes later, shortly followed by the cat, and then by Einstein, who was slower on account of having to hop from step to step.

'Do we really still have to go to school now that we have a penguin?' asked Arthur sleepily.

'Of course,' said Mrs Stewart. 'I'm sure little penguins have to go to school just like little people do.'

'I'm not little,' said Imogen, though this was mostly to herself.

'I don't want to go to school,' said Arthur, lifting Einstein up on to the chair between his own and Imogen's. It was stacked with a pile of books to help bring him up to table-height.

Einstein looked at Arthur and gave a concerned cluck.

'Arthur doesn't like school,' Imogen explained. 'He's only just started, and he doesn't have any friends yet.'

'*Imogen,*' Mrs Stewart scolded. 'Don't talk about your brother like that!'

'Sorry,' said Imogen. 'I didn't mean it in a bad way!'

Arthur rubbed his eyes groggily and started to

butter his toast, while Mrs Stewart flitted round the kitchen, trying to work out what penguins liked for breakfast.

'Just give him some more herring, Rachel,' said Mr Stewart tiredly.

'But he had that for supper *last* night!' Mrs Stewart sighed. 'Won't he get bored of eating the same thing?'

'He's a penguin, not a food critic,' said Mr Stewart. 'Put some chocolate spread on them if you think he wants garnish.'

Mrs Stewart sighed again, but went along with the idea. 'Imogen!' she cried, as she put Einstein's breakfast plate down in front of him. '*Try* not to get butter on the penguin!'

'I didn't mean to – I slipped!' said Imogen, who was now trying to scoop the butter off Einstein's head with her spoon, and put it back into the tub. Einstein didn't seem to notice, or care. He was too busy gobbling down the silver fish.

'Well, he seems to like the herrings!' said Mrs Stewart, who spotted the spoon and intercepted it before darting over to the kettle to make coffee.

'I'm not surprised, dear,' said Mr Stewart. 'He's a penguin.'

'Well, you know,' said Mrs Stewart vaguely. 'I'm sure they all have different tastes, and that sort of thing.'

Mr Stewart stopped chewing his toast for a moment, and turned to Arthur, frowning. 'Hang on, did that penguin sleep in your room last night?'

Arthur nodded. 'I was reading him a bedtime story.'

'You can't read,' said Imogen.

'Yes I can!' said Arthur.

'Is that hygienic?' asked Mr Stewart.

Mrs Stewart shrugged. 'Einstein seems clean enough,' she said, which, given the butter and the chocolate and the herrings, was no longer strictly true. 'And the cat sleeps where he likes, doesn't he?'

'Einstein will sleep downstairs tomorrow,' said Mr Stewart decidedly. 'Bedtime stories can be done in the sitting room.'

'What about while we're at school and you're at work?' asked Imogen.

'Can he come to school with us?' asked Arthur.

Mr Stewart frowned. He'd forgotten to think about that.

'Einstein will have to stay at home,' he said eventually. 'We'll leave some water in the bathtub, and put some herrings out on the table. Now, let's sort it out quickly because we're *all* running late.'

The usual leaving-the-house rush ensued. Imogen's second sock was retrieved from the larder, Gizmo was rescued from the laundry basket, and Einstein was given a pat on the head and left in the kitchen.

'Bye, Einstein!' said Imogen sadly as Mrs Stewart frantically tried to brush her hair into a ponytail. 'We'll be back again later!'

'I'll drive you to school,' said Mr Stewart, checking his watch as everybody rushed outside. 'You've run out of time to catch the bus. Car! Now!'

Everyone jumped in. The doors slammed shut and the car started to pull out of the driveway. Then,

'Arthur! Where's Arthur?' cried Mrs Stewart.

'I'm here,' said Arthur, suddenly appearing on the gravel beside the car, and slinging his bag over his shoulder. He opened the door and hopped in.

'Where did you go?' said Mr Stewart, narrowing his eyes.

'I left something in the kitchen.' Arthur gave an innocent little smile and adjusted the zips on his backpack.

Mr Stewart shrugged and started to drive.

*

When Arthur walked into the classroom for maths that morning, he felt twice as tall as usual. He chose a table in the middle of the room and tucked his backpack carefully between his feet. Then, as he waited for class to start, he leaned down and undid the zip slightly. Two shiny grey eyes blinked happily up at him.

'Make sure you keep quiet,' whispered Arthur. 'And stay in the bag, okay?'

The first half of the lesson went smoothly. Einstein didn't make a peep, aside from one small snore somewhere in the middle of the three times table; but as soon as Mr Smith started testing the class he woke up, and gave a sharp wriggle.

'Shh,' Arthur whispered. 'I know it's boring, but there's only ten minutes left.' He said it so quietly, however, that he wasn't sure Einstein could hear him.

'What's two times four?' Mr Smith asked, eyeing Arthur severely.

Arthur looked up from his backpack, and stared blankly at the whiteboard. 'Uh,' he said. 'Ten.' Einstein gave a lurch, and pecked him repeatedly on the ankle. 'I mean eight.'

'Good. So what's eight divided by two?'

Jack Jones, the boy who sat on Arthur's right, started to snigger.

Arthur felt his neck go hot. He didn't like being asked questions in front of the class, and Einstein was making it worse by moving about. Arthur couldn't think properly, and was just about to confess that he didn't know the answer when Einstein gave him four more pecks on the ankle.

Arthur paused, frowning. 'Four?' he guessed at last.

'Yes, exactly,' said Mr Smith, looking surprised. He turned to Arthur's neighbour. 'Layla, what's two times five?'

Arthur looked down at Einstein, who was staring up at him from inside the bag. 'Can you do maths?' he whispered incredulously.

Einstein ruffled his feathers smugly.

'Take your homework from the pile as you leave the room!' Mr Smith announced a few minutes later as the bell rang and the class started to file out of the room and in the direction of the playground. He looked down suspiciously as Arthur ducked past. 'And remember, everyone, homework should be your own work.'

Einstein soon settled down into the school routine.

Gizmo had almost always eaten Einstein's herrings by the time the Stewarts got home and, if Arthur ran upstairs quickly enough, he could leave Einstein splashing innocently around in the bathtub for somebody else to discover.

In fact, after just a few days, Arthur found it

difficult to remember what *not* having a penguin in his backpack used to feel like. It was comforting carrying Einstein around with his books and pencils. He kept the backpack unzipped slightly. When his family was looking the other way, Einstein could poke his head out and admire all the parts of London he hadn't seen before, and surprise old ladies on the bus. And, whenever Einstein had to keep his head *in*side the backpack, Arthur could walk around, knowing he had a secret, and it made him feel important.

Although maths was boring, the scariest part of the day, in Arthur's opinion, was lunch. Lucinda the dinner lady never seemed to smile, and she made Arthur feel as if he had done something very wrong just by coming to get food from her. He hated the sloppiness of the overcooked vegetables, and the fact that he couldn't leave the table without eating them. And, scariest of all, he never knew where to sit. Sometimes Imogen would let Arthur sit with *her* friends, but there wasn't always room, and she wasn't always eating at the same time as him. She preferred not to have her brother following her around anyway – not now that she was nine.

On the first Friday lunchtime since Einstein had moved in, Arthur took his fishfingers and chips from Lucinda, stammered a thank you and went to sit at a big table by himself, where he could pass chips to Einstein without anyone noticing, and stare at the cars going past outside the window. No one took backpacks into the lunch hall, so Arthur had transferred Einstein into his jacket in the secrecy of the changing room.

He had been feeding Einstein chips quite happily for several minutes when a voice took him by surprise. Arthur dropped the chip he was holding on to his plate and quickly shook his jacket, to warn Einstein to keep still.

The voice belonged to Theo, a new boy in Arthur's class who had lots of wavy black hair. 'Hello,' said Theo a second time, and sat down. 'You're Arthur, aren't you?'

Arthur nodded through a mouthful of squishy broccoli.

'I'm Theo,' said Theo.

'I know,' said Arthur, swallowing. 'You're in my class.'

'Yeah,' Theo grinned. 'You're the one who's good at maths!'

Einstein wriggled again, and Arthur's ears went pink. He had finished his food now, but Theo, beside him, was only just tucking into a great big fishfinger. Arthur buttoned up his jacket and hissed at Einstein to be quiet.

'What was that?' said Theo.

'Nothing,' said Arthur.

'Did you say "be quiet"?'

'No,' said Arthur. 'I said thank you.'

'Oh,' said Theo, through a mouthful of fish. 'That's okay.'

Arthur glanced down. Einstein had stopped moving, but his orange beak was poking out from the jacket as he eyed Theo's lunch.

'Einstein, *no*,' Arthur whispered sternly.

But it was too late. In a flurry of flippers, Einstein leaped out of Arthur's jacket, grabbed a fishfinger right off Theo's plate and disappeared with it under the table.

'Einstein!' shouted Arthur.

'What was *that*?' Theo leaped up in surprise and sent his plate and cutlery flying.

Imogen, who was just a few tables away, stared at them with wide eyes.

'*What is going on over there?*' Lucinda the dinner lady's voice echoed across the room. She came marching over, fish slice in hand, and glowered menacingly.

Arthur gulped. Einstein was still under the table, eating Theo's fish as if nothing was the matter. No one else seemed to have noticed him yet – no one except Theo and Imogen – but it wouldn't be long before they did.

'It was my fault!' said Theo suddenly.

Arthur stared at him.

'I don't like loud noises in my dining room,' said Lucinda loudly.

'I'm sorry,' said Theo. 'Arthur told me a very funny joke, which is why I shouted. And then I dropped my plate.' As he was talking, Theo nudged his jacket off his chair and on to the top of Einstein's head. It was a big jacket, and it covered Einstein neatly.

Lucinda narrowed her eyes. 'Jokes,' she said slowly, 'should be told *quietly*, if at all.'

'Sorry,' said Theo a second time. 'It won't happen again.'

Lucinda scowled again, as if she knew something was amiss, but couldn't tell what. She retreated reluctantly to her kitchen.

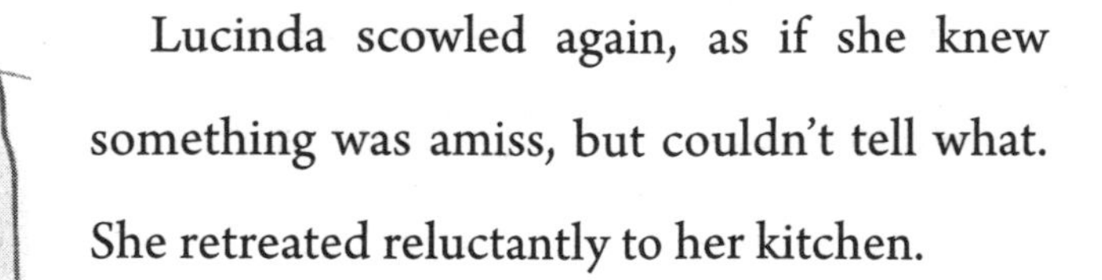

With Lucinda a safe distance away, Theo crouched down and scooped up Einstein, bundling him up inside the jacket, and turned to look at Arthur. The two boys grinned at each other and hurried out of the dining room.

Arthur and Theo ran as fast as they could to the end of the playground, where they couldn't be seen from the school. Theo placed his jacket down on the ground and Einstein came tumbling out of it, his beak still full of fishfinger. He hopped up and shook his flippers for balance.

'You have a penguin!' said Theo at last.

'His name's Einstein,' said Arthur. 'Thanks for covering for us.'

'Where did you find him?'

Arthur hesitated for a moment. 'At the zoo,' he said. 'He followed us home.'

'That's the coolest thing I've ever heard!' said Theo.

'He's been in my backpack all week, actually,' said Arthur. Then, panicking for a moment, he added, 'Do you promise not to tell anyone?'

'It's okay,' said Theo. 'I won't.'

He spat on his hand and held it out for Arthur to shake, and Arthur – a little confused because he'd never seen anyone do that before – did the same.

Just then Imogen appeared outside the dining hall and came marching across the playground towards them.

'Uh-oh,' said Arthur under his breath.

'What?'

'It's my sister. Hide the penguin again.'

'So you've been taking Einstein to school, have you?' said Imogen, as soon as she was within earshot. She raised an eyebrow and crossed her arms, just like their mother did when she was cross.

'No,' said Arthur.

'Yes you have.'

'How do you know?'

'Because his foot is poking out from underneath your friend's jacket.'

Theo looked embarrassed and tried to nudge the jacket over the stray foot.

'Well, I've seen him now,' said Imogen, 'so you might as well admit it.'

'Don't tell Dad,' Arthur pleaded.

Imogen pursed her lips and thought for a moment. 'Okay, but I want shotgun in the car for the next month,' she said.

'What? You can't do that!'

'So I can tell Mum and Dad?'

'Okay,' said Arthur. '*Fine.*'

'See you at home time!' said Imogen sweetly, and she disappeared back across the playground.

Chapter Five

# A New Friend and a Lost One

The weekend was snowy.

It was a bright, bossy sort of snow, with great big flakes that fell slowly and softly like the sky really meant them. The sort of light, white winter's day when noises are muffled and London seems ready to burst with happiness at simply being awake.

Breakfast had occurred without incident, snowballs had been born off the window ledges, and Imogen was curled up on her favourite cushion, with a pile of detective books and a telescope. She had read most of these books already, but she'd never much liked the idea of carrying *one* book around without any of its friends, or of having *one* thing kept neatly when she could have a great big messy pile of stuff instead.

The current book was a mystery about a stolen painting, and Imogen was enjoying it very much. The main character was a detective called Inspector Bucket, who was very clever, and always found clues in the places you'd least expect them. At the end of each page she would turn to the window to check that it was still snowing, or look through the telescope to see if it made the flakes look bigger – it mostly just made them look blurry.

Arthur was playing outside with his new friend, and Imogen wasn't sure how she felt about it. She had played with them too, for a bit, but usually when she played with Arthur she could make the rules. Now that Theo had joined in, they were throwing the snowballs too hard, and hadn't been interested in making snow angels. And so Imogen had decided all at once that, being nine, she was much too grown up for both brothers *and* snow, and had come inside to hide in the house.

Imogen's favourite cushion was in the upstairs corridor, next to a round window that looked out over the garden, where the boys were cheering as Einstein slid around on his belly. Imogen watched them through her telescope.

Then, remembering that she wasn't interested in that sort of thing, she pointed the telescope upwards and examined the roofs on the houses across the street instead. When she looked back down a moment later, the boys were over by the garden wall, and Einstein had disappeared.

A sudden bouncing of feet up the stairs seemed to answer her confusion, and she turned to see Einstein waddling down the corridor towards her.

Imogen, pleased as she was to see him, looked at

Einstein suspiciously. She'd been feeling a little hard done by: Arthur had seen Einstein first, and Arthur had taken him to school, and Arthur had been able to introduce him to his friends, and Einstein probably preferred Arthur too. Imogen's friends didn't know about Einstein – and how could she tell them if Einstein was never hidden in her backpack to prove it?

Einstein looked at her sincerely and stretched his flippers out, like he did before a particularly large squawk.

Imogen smiled despite herself. 'Hello, Einstein,' she said.

Einstein looked visibly relieved, and gave a smaller, softer squawk, as if to ask her how she was.

'I'm reading books about detectives,' said Imogen. 'Some of them have very long words, but I can understand them anyway.'

He tilted his head to one side, the way he did when he didn't understand something.

'Detectives are people who solve mysteries,' Imogen explained. 'They use clues to look for lost things.'

Einstein seemed interested in this, so she handed him one of the books.

'Here,' she said. 'Have a look.'

He leaned over and peered down his beak at the front cover. Then he turned the book over with his foot, and read the back.

'That's one of my favourites,' said Imogen. 'It's about a kidnapping. Oh – a kidnapping is when baddies steal someone away, and ask for lots of money to return them.'

Einstein looked up at her and his little eyes widened.

'But don't worry!' said Imogen. 'Inspector Bucket always gets them back.'

Einstein gave a terrified honk, and then waddle-ran as fast as he could back along the corridor and down the stairs. Imogen watched him go. 'Silly penguin,' she said to herself, and carried on reading.

Einstein made a point of sitting next to Imogen at lunch. He waddled up to the chair beside her and bossily squawked to be lifted up.

'We should get him a high chair, really,' said Mrs Stewart.

'*That* implies you think he's staying here forever,' said Mr Stewart tetchily as he balanced Einstein on his usual pile of books.

'You wanted him to stay forever first!' said Mrs Stewart. 'And I'm sorry you're so cross, but I've told you your work trousers will dry-clean.'

'We can't afford to dry-clean our clothes every day for*ever*, Rachel,' Mr Stewart grumbled.

'And we won't! He's making very good progress with his toilet training!'

'He *can* hear you, you know!' cried Imogen

defensively. She turned to look at Einstein and noticed he was holding a piece of paper in his beak, which he placed on the table in front of her.

'He's never *once* made a mess while the children have been at school, has he?' Mrs Stewart went on vaguely.

Imogen picked the paper up to inspect it.

'What did he just give you?' asked Arthur, who had, until that moment, been busily talking to Theo about superheroes.

'It's just another of Einstein's photos of himself,' said Imogen.

Einstein gave an urgent little caw.

'What?' she asked him. 'Isn't it you?' She looked back at the photograph and noticed the little strands of yellow feathers splaying out from the penguin's eyebrows, as well as its reddish eyes, which differed from Einstein's dark ones. 'Oh,' she said. 'It's *not* you.' She turned the photograph over and saw that the

name ISAAC was written rather messily on the bottom corner.

'Soup's ready!' Mr Stewart cried. 'Put that away, Imogen.'

Imogen shoved the photograph into her pocket and gave Einstein a quick little smile, to show him that she wouldn't forget about it.

'I don't like soup,' whinged Arthur. 'We *al*ways have soup.'

'You can learn to like soup,' said Mr Stewart, placing one bowl down in front of him, and another in front of Theo.

'Einstein doesn't like soup, either,' Imogen pointed out. 'It gets in his eyes when he tries to drink it.'

'Oh, yes . . .' said Mrs Stewart. 'Do you think he'd prefer a Pot Noodle?'

'Hey!' said Arthur. '*That*'s not fair!'

'Just give him another raw herring,' said Mr Stewart tiredly. 'And, Arthur, if you complain about my cooking again, then you can have a raw herring too.'

Theo almost spilled his soup from giggling.

Einstein followed Imogen around all afternoon. He stayed beside her for the whole of their walk on the heath, and watched her while she fidgeted over her science homework, and hardly noticed when the boys tried to convince him to play catch with them.

Imogen was both confused and flattered. She didn't smell of herrings or sardines – she even sniffed herself to check – and she looked just the same as usual.

'Why is Einstein staring at you?' said Arthur. He and Theo had come back inside, disappointed by Einstein's disinterest in their games.

'I don't know.' Imogen shrugged. 'He's been doing

it ever since he gave me that photo at lunch.'

Einstein squawked at her, so Imogen took the photo back out of her pocket and looked at it.

'Did you see him before lunch?' asked Theo. 'He disappeared.'

'Yes, he came upstairs to look at my detective books.'

Imogen frowned: it was the mention of detectives and kidnappings that had made Einstein start acting strangely. 'I think the penguin in the photo must be a friend of his or something. He's called Isaac.'

'How do you know his name?' asked Arthur, peering at the photo. 'Isaac,' he read. 'Einstein, did you write that?'

Einstein blinked and nodded.

'Cool!' said Arthur. 'I bet no one else has a penguin who can write!'

Then Theo leaned over Imogen's shoulder and had a look at the photo. 'I like his yellow eyebrows,' he said. 'Where's your friend now, Einstein?'

Einstein squawked again, and shrugged his flippers.

'You don't know?' said Arthur.

Imogen's eyes widened, and suddenly everything fell into place. 'That's right!' she cried. 'His friend must be missing! That's why he was scared when I mentioned kidnappings!'

Einstein quickly nodded his head.

'Perhaps he's been kidnapped and held for ransom by pirates!' she went on excitedly, prompting another scared honk from Einstein. 'Sorry, Einstein – I didn't really mean that . . . But don't worry! We'll get Isaac back.'

Einstein nudged one of Imogen's books towards her, and poked the name on the front cover with his beak.

'Oh, no – Inspector Bucket isn't a real detective,' she explained.

Einstein hung his flippers in disappointment.

'But *I'll* help you!' said Imogen. She tried to speak in a way that was both determined and comforting, just like Inspector Bucket did in her books. 'Arthur, you can be my assistant. Fetch my notebook and magnifying glass!'

'I don't know where they are,' said Arthur. 'Your room's always too messy to find anything.'

'Have you looked at all his other photos?' asked Theo helpfully.

'I think so,' said Imogen, going a little pink at her overenthusiasm, but she agreed that they ought to check.

Theo picked up Einstein's backpack from where it was lying on the floor and started rooting through the pockets.

'We've already seen all of those,' said Arthur, leaning over Theo's shoulder.

Then Theo pulled a different photo out of a different pocket, and turned it over. 'What about this one?'

The new photo showed a pile of wooden crates sitting beside a lorry. One of them had two little holes in the side, and peering through the holes – just visible between the shadows – was a pair of eyes. Eyes surrounded by feathery yellow eyebrows. The box was labelled in black paint: **UK**.

Imogen gasped, and Arthur grabbed the photo out of Theo's hand.

'UK?' he read aloud.

'United Kingdom,' Imogen explained. Then she tried to grab the photo from Arthur.

'I know what UK means,' said Arthur crossly, though in actual fact he had been a little too excited to remember. He pushed his sister's hand away. 'It doesn't say where in the UK, though. His friend could be anywhere! Do you think someone kidnapped him from the beach in Australia?'

'Give it here!' said Imogen, leaping at him.

'Stop it!' cried Theo. 'Look at Einstein! You're upsetting him.'

Imogen and Arthur stopped bickering and turned round. Einstein had ruffled up his feathers and was staring down at the surface of the table, hunching his back sadly.

'Now look what you've done!' said Imogen. 'He's upset!'

'It wasn't *my* fault!' said Arthur.

'It's okay, Einstein,' said Imogen. She leaned down and looked him carefully in the eye. 'We're going to help you find him,' she said. 'We promise.'

## Chapter Six

# Detectives at Work

The woman in the café held the poster at arm's length and frowned at it through her reading glasses. 'Do you have an adult with you?' she asked, looking down at Arthur over the countertop. 'You need an adult with you if you want to put a poster on the noticeboard.'

'He's only six,' said Imogen, stepping away from the cupcakes she had been admiring in the window and putting a hand on her brother's arm. 'But I'll be ten in March. Does that count?'

The waitress glanced at the messy-haired girl in the red duffel coat, and was just about to say something clever when she spotted the penguin poking out of her right-hand pocket. 'But – but—' She shook the poster at them frantically. 'Your penguin's right there,' she squeaked, pointing at Imogen's coat.

Imogen took the poster back from the waitress and placed it down on the counter, so that Arthur's crayon rendition of Isaac's yellow eyebrows stared alarmingly up at the café ceiling. 'It's a *different* penguin,' said Imogen, pointing out the colours, and then running her finger along her own handwriting for emphasis:

Missing Pengwin, Possibly Kid-Napped,
Informashion To Be Rewarded.

'See?' she added politely. 'The penguin *we* want is missing, but *this* penguin isn't missing at all!'

The waitress shook her head in disbelief. The café didn't have any rules about penguins. No cats, no dogs, no political leaflets on the noticeboard – but penguins? 'All right, fine,' she said tiredly. 'I'll put it up. Can I take a name, in case anyone responds?'

'DCI Imogen Stewart,' said Imogen. 'And this is my assistant, Arthur.'

'Thank you for your help,' said Arthur, his ears going pink.

'See you again soon,' said Imogen, and then she paused. 'Actually, can we have three of those cupcakes too, please?' She scooped some change out of her pocket and fumbled around with it on the counter. 'One pound, nearly two . . .' she mumbled, as the waitress waited and watched Einstein nervously. 'I think I've got some more change in my other pocket. Is it all right if I take my penguin out so I can have a look?'

'You know what? Have the third cupcake for free,'

said the waitress, placing them down on the counter. 'I'm sure you have lots more posters to hand out, and I wouldn't want to hold you up.'

'Thank you!' said Imogen, beaming, and she took the cupcakes and followed her brother out on to the street.

They sat on the bench outside to eat their cupcakes. Einstein's cupcake was too big for him to eat in one go, so Imogen broke it up into little pieces and threw them into the air for him to catch. Several passers-by stopped and stared, and once or twice some pigeons got in the way – but Einstein would chase them until they flew up on to the café awning to watch from above instead.

'Well done, Einstein!' cried Imogen, clapping, as he grabbed a piece of icing that was about to land in front of another particularly

fat pigeon. Yesterday's snow was still on the ground around them, going grey in slushy heaps at the edge of the road. Imogen kicked it about with her boots as they walked off.

'Shall we put a poster up in the bus stop?' asked Arthur.

'Good idea,' said Imogen. She turned round to see Einstein on the verge of a fight with another pigeon, so handed her brother the posters before running over to rescue him. 'Stop it, Einstein,' she scolded, and put him back into her pocket. 'That one's bigger than you!'

Einstein squawked sulkily, and glared at the pigeon from the safety of the duffel coat as it swaggered away down the road.

They taped the posters up and down all the parts of town they knew, and kept going until they had run out of posters entirely. Some went in shops, others on signposts, and the biggest was saved for the noticeboard outside the library. Imogen felt particularly proud as she pinned this one up because it was so big, and colourful, and it had her neatest handwriting on it. The name 'Isaac' had been written by Einstein, with a pencil held uncertainly in his beak. Then Imogen had gone over it more neatly with a pen.

She took her detective notebook out of her pocket and put a big tick next to where she had written Missing Penguin Posters. ✔

The snow restarted as they walked home, coughed down in little spatters by a greying sky and then gathering speed. Big flakes were soon sticking in Imogen's hair and falling down inside Arthur's collar. Einstein nestled further into Imogen's coat pocket and hid his head from sight.

'Do you think we'll find Isaac?' said Arthur.

'Of course!' said Imogen confidently, because she was the oldest. But she was starting to feel less confident with every step. Pinning the posters up had felt like *doing* something. She hadn't thought about what might happen *after* it was done: anything could, or maybe nothing would.

'Before Christmas?' said Arthur.

Einstein poked his head back out of Imogen's pocket for a moment, and blinked at her.

Imogen frowned. Christmas wasn't far away now: there was only a week left of school, and then only a few days of holiday before the day itself. And they couldn't search for Isaac while they were busy at school, could they? They'd be in lessons. They could ask their parents for help – but Mr Stewart often got cross enough about having just *one* penguin about the house. He'd never let Isaac stay too, even if they could find him. And then maybe Einstein wouldn't want to live with them any more.

‘Before Christmas,’ Imogen agreed. ‘I’m absolutely sure of it.’

Mr Stewart narrowed his eyes as the children entered the kitchen. ‘Where have you two been?’

‘We were playing in the garden,’ said Arthur.

‘For a whole hour?’ said Mr Stewart. ‘Together? Without arguing?’

‘And we bought cupcakes from the café,’ said Imogen.

‘You shouldn’t leave the garden by yourselves,’ said Mrs Stewart, glancing up from her pile of marking.

‘It’s only across the road!’ said Imogen.

‘Don’t argue with your mother.’

‘Sorry,’ Imogen mumbled. She took her coat off and placed Einstein down on the floor, where he gave a satisfied chunter and shook the few snowflakes that had lodged themselves in his feathers in a shower down on to the carpet.

Mr Stewart smiled despite himself.

'Where's all my paper gone?' said Mrs Stewart.

'No idea,' said Mr Stewart, turning back to his laptop. 'Never saw it.'

'I had a great big pile of paper right next to the printer! Just this morning!'

The children looked at each other and sidled up the stairs into Arthur's bedroom.

Imogen paced up and down beside Arthur's bed. She scratched her head and tried putting her hands behind her back, and then inside her pockets, and then behind her back again.

'Come on, *think*!' she said, to no one in particular.

'I don't know what I'm supposed to be thinking about,' said Arthur, who was sitting on a beanbag with Einstein, sticking Lego pieces together into a tower.

Imogen didn't know, either, but she wasn't going to let on. 'This is important,' she insisted. 'Einstein needs to find his friend. It's why he's here!'

'Is it?' said Arthur.

Einstein gave a small squawk of agreement.

'I thought you were here because you liked us,' said Arthur, sounding crestfallen.

'He *does* like you, Arthur,' said Imogen. 'But we like him too. And we promised that we'd find his friend. And people who like each other keep their promises. Where's my magnifying glass?'

Arthur picked the magnifying glass up from underneath a cushion and handed it to his sister, who started closely examining Isaac's photograph for the eleventh time that day. She had glued the photo into the first page of her notebook and added lots of arrows around its edges. They formed a spider diagram like the ones she had seen the police do on TV, all leading to lots of important notes: things like:

Arthur took his own photo out of his pocket, and looked at it again. It turned out Einstein had had several photos of Isaac – enough for Arthur and Imogen to borrow one each. Still, Arthur wasn't sure what staring at a photo all day could do: it wasn't like they ever changed shape or told you anything different. He put it back into his pocket and went on playing with his Lego.

'I've got the facts, but they just don't add together,'

said Imogen mysteriously. She turned to look out of the window, where the snow had stopped falling and the sky had settled down to darkness. 'Interesting,' she mumbled to herself.

Suddenly Mr Stewart opened the door. 'What are you kids up to?' he said.

Imogen jumped and spun round, quickly tucking her magnifying glass into her back pocket. 'Nothing,' she said.

Mr Stewart turned to the sofa and looked at Arthur, who shrugged, and then at Einstein, who looked blank and tripped over a pillow.

'I know you're up to something,' he said. 'I've never seen you go this long without fighting.'

'It's Einstein,' said Imogen, smiling sweetly. 'He brings us together.'

They all turned to look at the little penguin, who was now face down on the sofa, struggling to push himself up with his flippers. Arthur quickly lifted him on to his feet.

'Hmm,' said Mr Stewart. 'All right. Supper's in ten minutes, so wash your hands . . . and wash that penguin's flippers while you're at it too.'

Imogen felt worse again during supper. Mr Stewart had made her favourite roast chicken, but it was going down all wrong, and her stomach was doing guilty somersaults every time she looked over at Einstein happily eating his herrings. What if she *never* found Isaac? Maybe she had got too far ahead of herself with all those detective promises. She would break Einstein's heart. What could a nine-year-old do to change anything, after all? Maybe Isaac *had* been kidnapped and held for ransom by pirates, and even if Imogen managed to work out what ship he was on she was much too small to beat anyone in a sword fight, and would probably be kidnapped and held for ransom herself. And then who would rescue *her*? She wasn't a detective, she was just a silly little—

'Imogen?' said Mrs Stewart kindly.

'Huh, what?' said Imogen, through a mouthful of potato.

'I was just asking how you'd got on with your science homework? You're miles away!'

'Oh,' said Imogen. 'Yeah. It was easy.'

'Jolly good,' said Mrs Stewart, and turned to Einstein. 'Would you like some gravy with your herrings, dear?'

Mr Stewart rolled his eyes gently. 'What are you thinking about, hmm?' he asked Imogen.

She caught her brother's eye across the table. 'Nothing,' she said quickly.

'You look worried.'

'Oh – I was just thinking about school tomorrow. We have a spelling test.'

'You're good at spelling, aren't you?'

'I'm okay,' said Imogen, stirring a piece of broccoli round her plate with her fork. 'Science is easier.'

'Well! Only a week to go – and then it's the Christmas holidays!'

Imogen smiled.

'Can Einstein stay for Christmas?' asked Arthur.

'Of course!' said Mrs Stewart.

'Well –' Mr Stewart coughed – 'I think we should all remember that Einstein's stay is still on a temporary, take-each-day-as-it-comes basis, just until we work out where he actually lives . . .'

His sentence trailed off: Einstein was blinking at Mr Stewart from the other side of the table, over the top of the white napkin that Mrs Stewart had fixed round his neck for herring spillages.

'But, you know,' Mr Stewart went on vaguely, 'if Christmas comes along and it suits everyone for Einstein to be here, then, well, there's no *specific* reason why not.'

'*Yes!*' Arthur whispered to himself, and Einstein gave a small herring-breathed squawk.

'Can he have his own stocking?' Arthur went on. 'Do you think he'll like Christmas pudding?'

'And *on that note*!' Mr Stewart interrupted. 'It is a school night, and you both need to get ready for bed.'

Imogen looked out of the bathroom window while she brushed her teeth.

The pavement outside was only dimly lit, shadowy beneath the glow that fell from the windows. When she pressed her face against the glass, it felt cold, and little white shadows of fog appeared. She wiped them away with the sleeve of her dressing gown.

Their first poster was dangling forlornly from a battered old lamp post, where the Stewarts' street met the corner of the next street along. Imogen frowned at it. It didn't seem like much use all of a sudden.

Then, just as she was about to turn to spit into the basin, she saw somebody approach it. Imogen gasped despite herself and nearly swallowed her toothpaste.

She couldn't see the somebody's face, but she could see that they were wearing a long white coat, and a strange, wide-brimmed hat.

She watched as a large hand reached up to the poster, examined it for a moment and pulled it down. Then the somebody folded the poster into their pocket and, as if reacting to her presence, looked up at Imogen's bedroom window. For a split second, she could make out a man's face, and she ducked down beneath the curtains.

When Imogen looked back a few moments later, the man was gone.

## Chapter Seven

# Arthur's Revenge

The school playing fields were always muddy when it rained, and it had rained all week: that particularly cross sort of rain that melts the snow and then the grass beneath it too. The Year Two boys had spent the last hour doing football drills.

'Line up in your teams and practise passing!'

Mr Burnett, the coach, was standing at the edge of the football pitch in a full tracksuit, clutching a flask of hot coffee. 'Come on, Arthur!' he said. 'It isn't that cold!'

Arthur gave a particularly violent shiver and tried to dribble the ball towards his partner.

'You can go faster than that!' Mr Burnett cried.

Jack Jones sniggered and shoved Arthur out of the way. 'Move,' he said, and then dribbled the ball away across the grass, stopping here and there to bounce it in the air from foot to foot.

Arthur folded his arms. His trainers were muddy, and so were his knees. He was so muddy he felt like he might turn into mud, and have to squelch about on the football pitch for the rest of his life. At least mud didn't have to play football, though, so maybe it would be all right – as long as he didn't get stuck to Jack Jones's knees or anything like that.

'Are you okay?'

It was Theo.

'I'm fine,' said Arthur.

'Where's Einstein?' asked Theo.

'He's hiding inside. The mud messes up his feathers.

And I think he's still sad about his friend.'

Jack kicked the ball back to Arthur hard, so that it bashed him in the shins.

'Sir, sir! Arthur's not concentrating!' Jack whined.

'Arthur Stewart!' said Mr Burnett, marching over to stare down at him through a cloud of coffee steam. 'You might just be the worst footballer I've ever seen.'

Arthur looked down at his shoes and tried to laugh. 'Sorry, sir,' he mumbled.

'Don't worry,' whispered Theo. 'He said that to my brother last week.'

Then Mr Burnett blew his orange whistle and started shouting. 'Right! Inside! Change and shower! Arthur, collect the cones! Jack, you're on balls! Theo, you help them out!'

A few minutes later, Arthur, Theo and Jack Jones were heading inside together through the drizzle. Most of the other boys had finished changing and were starting to disappear from the cloakroom, which was damp and smelly now, with clumps of mud all over the floor.

'Hi, Einstein,' said Theo very quietly.

Einstein was hiding inside Arthur's kitbag, doing his best not to squawk at the dirty football socks that had suddenly appeared beside him.

Arthur grinned, and opened the bag just wide enough for Theo to give Einstein a quick pat on the head.

'What are you two looking at?' said Jack.

Arthur zipped the bag up and turned round. 'Nothing.'

'*Nothing,*' Jack imitated. 'What's in your bag?'

Theo and Arthur glanced at each other.

'It's just a photo,' said Theo. 'Nothing interesting.'

'Let me see,' said Jack.

Arthur tried not to make eye contact. 'No,' he said.

'Why not?' Jack asked. 'If it's just a photo, why can't I see it?'

'Just show him the picture,' Theo whispered.

Arthur frowned. He didn't suppose it would do any harm, and it might stop Jack grabbing the bag off him and finding Einstein. He reached into the pocket of his backpack and pulled out the second Polaroid of Isaac.

Jack grabbed it. He frowned, and then sniggered. 'You keep a photo of a penguin at a zoo in your pocket? You're so weird.' He shoved the photo back into Arthur's hands and retreated to his corner of the changing room.

Arthur stared dumbly at the floor. 'A zoo . . .' he whispered to himself. Of course, the photo of Isaac had *obviously* been taken at a zoo. The water in the background didn't look natural at all. He'd been so distracted by what Isaac looked like in the photo that he'd forgotten to think about where it had actually been taken. He'd have to tell Imogen.

Arthur washed the dirt off his legs and got dressed

quickly. It was almost the end of the school day. In just a few minutes he'd be able to go home, and not have to worry about anything – not maths, not Jack Jones, not football, not Mr Burnett – for three entire weeks, until January. And, come January, Arthur felt convinced that he'd be far too grown up to ever need to worry about anything again.

He put his bag over his shoulder, waited for Theo to finish changing and turned to leave.

'Nice glasses,' someone sniggered.

It was Jack again. Arthur ignored him.

'Where are you two going?' asked Jack.

'Home,' said Arthur. He felt Einstein give an angry wriggle inside his bag.

'Are you going to tell your mummy I was mean to you?' Jack teased.

'Go away, Jack,' said Arthur quietly.

He hated it when this happened. He didn't like Jack, either, so what did it matter if Jack didn't like him? But

Jack always had quick things to say, and Arthur never did. His brain would stop working and his neck would go hot, and then he'd look stupid and babyish, just like Jack said he was.

'Crybaby,' Jack sniggered, and he pushed past to leave first.

'Unzip the bag,' whispered Theo.

'What?' said Arthur.

Einstein was still wriggling desperately from somewhere underneath Arthur's dirty football kit.

'Unzip it,' said Theo again.

Arthur shrugged and did as Theo said. No sooner had he opened it than Einstein burst from the bag and leaped spectacularly through the air – right towards Jack's head.

'Aaah!' Jack screamed, covering his face with his hands. 'Get off! Get off!'

Einstein had landed on Jack's shoulder and was angrily pecking his ears.

'What is it? Get it off me!' cried Jack as Einstein squawked and batted him over the head with his flippers.

The door of the changing room burst open. Hearing the footsteps, Einstein hopped down to the ground. Theo scooped him up and quickly hid him back inside Arthur's kitbag.

Mr Burnett came striding round the corner, his mouth already going flat at the corners like it did when he was about to tell someone off. 'What's going on in here, then?'

'It was Arthur!' Jack whimpered.

Arthur blinked nervously.

'Arthur?' said Mr Burnett sternly. 'What did you do?'

'Nothing,' said Arthur, not strictly telling a lie. 'I was just standing here.'

'There was a penguin!' said Jack desperately. 'He attacked me with a penguin!'

'A penguin?' Mr Burnett looked blankly from Arthur to Theo, as if waiting for one of them to fill him in.

'I don't know what he's talking about,' said Arthur. 'He just started yelling.'

Theo shrugged. 'I didn't see a penguin, either, sir. Do you think maybe he needs to go to the nurse?'

Mr Burnett frowned and shook his head. 'Get out, all of you.'

'I'm not making it up!' said Jack. 'He made a penguin appear!'

'That is *enough*!' said Mr Burnett, pleased at finally having something to raise his voice to. 'No more talking nonsense, or you'll be waiting on the edge of the pitch during football next term.'

'Sorry,' Jack mumbled, quickly falling silent. He picked his bag up from where he had dropped it and hurried out of the room.

'Maybe I'll start talking nonsense too if that's the punishment,' said Arthur to Theo, as they followed Jack outside.

It was still drizzling out in the playground, and the grey clouds had drooped a little closer to the ground. Arthur put his hood up as they walked towards the crowd of parents who were waiting, under a swarm of umbrellas, at the gates.

Just then Imogen came bursting out of the door of the library and hurried over to join them. Her hair was looking messier than usual, and she was clutching her ragged notebook to her chest.

'Hello,' she said, falling into step beside her brother.

'Hi?' said Arthur. Imogen was using her mysterious voice again.

'I've made several new discoveries,' she whispered.

'I'll explain everything when I can.'

'So have I!' said Arthur, pleased to finally be of use. 'Why can't you explain everything now?'

'Because we don't know who's listening!' Imogen gave the empty pavement a significant glance, shoved her notebook into her coat pocket and darted off again, as if she didn't really know them.

'Is your sister okay?' asked Theo.

Arthur shrugged. 'I don't know. She was acting crazy at breakfast too. It's about this friend of Einstein's.'

Einstein gave a sudden, sad little caw from inside Arthur's bag.

'Well?' said Imogen, shortly after supper that evening.

Just like they always did on the first night of the holidays, Imogen and Arthur had chosen a Christmas film to watch with their favourite pudding, which was apple crumble and ice cream. Mr Stewart had paused *The Grinch* and headed into the kitchen in order to pour what must have been his eleventh cup of tea.

'Well, what?' said Arthur.

'Well, what was your discovery?'

'I think Einstein and Isaac must have come from a zoo,' Arthur whispered, as their father sat back down in his armchair and pressed PLAY again on the remote control.

Imogen frowned. 'But Einstein's from Australia.'

'Aren't there zoos in Australia?'

Imogen hadn't thought about that. She'd been imagining vast plains and dramatic beaches.

'The background in the photo doesn't look natural,' Arthur went on.

'You might be right,' Imogen admitted. She actually sounded impressed.

'And what was your discovery?' Arthur asked.

Imogen thought about the man she had seen on the street outside. It hardly seemed real now, in front of the telly with her family all around her. Maybe she'd been dreaming, after all – and anyway she didn't want

Arthur worrying about it and telling their parents.

'Nothing yet,' she said quietly. 'I'm still thinking.'

'Oh,' said Arthur. 'Well, shall we tell Mum and Dad that we think Einstein's from a zoo?'

'No,' said Imogen sharply. 'Dad will want to send him back to it.'

'Shh,' said Mr Stewart, and Einstein – who was sitting on his lap – gave them a stroppy little squawk too. 'We're trying to watch *The Grinch*.'

Imogen and Arthur looked at each other and tried not to giggle.

They stayed like that for the rest of the film. Mr Stewart didn't even look cross when Einstein fell asleep and started to snore like a foghorn, and Imogen watched them and thought about how maybe – just maybe – if Mr Stewart was getting used to Einstein, he would get used to a second penguin too, and everything would be okay.

Their parents let them stay awake for a whole hour beyond their usual bedtime. Then, spotting the time on the clock above the fireplace, Mrs Stewart clapped her hands together and cried, 'Quick – straight to bed! Or you'll be much too tired for our shopping trip tomorrow.'

As they walked up the stairs, Arthur managed to give Imogen a brief, whispered, blow-by-blow account of Einstein's daring battle with Jack Jones.

'If Mr Burnett hadn't come in, he would probably

have killed him,' Arthur exaggerated, and, in the dazed sleepiness brought on by apple crumble, he almost believed it.

*

Christmas holidays or not, Imogen couldn't sleep.

She could hear Arthur snoring next door, and her parents listening to the news downstairs with the volume low. The streetlamps outside were casting narrow shadows through the blinds the way they always did after lights-out. Imogen stared up at the ceiling, with all its luminous star stickers and bits of old Blu-tack, and thought about Isaac again.

What would a *real* detective do? She had put up posters, she had written everything she knew down in a notebook, she had looked at things through a magnifying glass – but what now? Isaac's crate hadn't even had a proper address on it: he could be anywhere in the UK. He could have been shipped off to another country altogether. What were the chances of someone identifying him from some posters on a few little streets in London? The strange man in the hat had seemed interested in their posters, of course – perhaps he knew something. Or perhaps he was an assassin, or a penguin-murderer, or whatever kind of person it is that stuffs animals before they go on display in museums.

'Check the newspapers!' she breathed suddenly, sitting up in bed.

How could she have been so stupid? It was what Inspector Bucket did when things went missing: he would check all the papers for any events that might give him some sort of clue – like when a painting went missing from a gallery in London, and he had found the thief trying to sell it through a newspaper advertisement in Bristol. Of course, it would be easier for Imogen because Inspector Bucket lived in the olden days and didn't have the internet.

She grabbed her notebook, jumped into her

fluffy slippers, and tiptoed down the corridor to the computer in Mrs Stewart's study.

Imogen sat down at her mother's desk, opened the laptop and bit her lip in thought. She tried typing **lost pengwin** into Google, but nothing useful came up – just a few silly-looking storybooks. Then she tried **missing pengwin**, **kidnapped pengwin** and **pengwin escape**. Several articles appeared:

**Penguin Escape Plan Foiled By Zoo Workers . . .**

**Penguin Stolen From Dublin Zoo Safely Returned . . .**

**Lost Penguin's Daring Escape From Sydney Zoo Filmed On . . .**

Imogen breathed in sharply. Sydney: that had been on Einstein's flight label. She opened the article and scrolled down the page:

# Lost Penguin's Daring Escape From Sydney Zoo Filmed On CCTV (27th November)

A little penguin from Sydney Zoo – known by his keepers as Einstein – managed to escape from Sydney Zoo on Wednesday. Zookeeper Ted Smith reported that Einstein had been visibly restless since the transportation of one of Sydney Zoo's rockhopper penguins to a zoo in the UK a few weeks beforehand. It is unclear whether this detail influenced Einstein's escape, but when a gate in the enclosure was left open during feeding time Einstein made a dash for freedom, and was quickly lost among the crowds. His initial escape from the penguin enclosure was caught on CCTV, but the zoo has so far been unable to find out how, and indeed if, he managed to escape from the zoo itself.

If anyone has any information relating to the location of Einstein the penguin, they should contact Sydney Zoo immediately. Einstein is particularly distinctive due to his orange beak, which differs from the standard dark beak of other little penguins. This mutation helps his zookeepers to recognise him.

Little penguins, otherwise known as fairy penguins, are the world's smallest penguin species, growing up to around 34 cm and weighing up to 1.4 kg . . .

*

So Arthur had been right.

Imogen's heart was pounding. She opened a new tab and quickly searched for **rockhopper pengwins UK**.

The first result was Edinburgh Zoo, the second London – but Einstein had been to London Zoo already. The penguins in the pictures had red eyes and spiky yellow eyebrows, just like Isaac's. One of them – the smallest – looked exactly like her photo, right down to the last feather. Could it be Isaac?

Imogen grabbed her notebook and scribbled down her findings, underlining Edinburgh, Sydney and Einstein in her mother's red biro.

'Rachel – you've left the light on in your study!' Mr Stewart's voice sounded from the staircase.

Imogen's eyes widened and she slammed the laptop shut.

'Oh, have I?' Mrs Stewart replied. 'Can you get it for me?'

'All right.' Her father's footsteps started to approach along the corridor.

Imogen jumped up from the desk and rushed over to the door, then stood with her back pressed against it, holding her breath as she thought of excuses.

*I forgot I needed to use the internet for my homework* – would that work? On the first night of the school holidays?

The creaky floorboard outside the door went *creak!* – and Imogen prepared herself for a telling-off – when suddenly—

'James! Can you help me find the front-door keys?' Mrs Stewart called up the stairs. 'I need to lock up.'

Mr Stewart paused. Imogen could hear him moving on the other side of the door, which was still slightly ajar.

His hand reached blindly through the gap and flicked the light switch beside her head, and then he turned round. She breathed out as she heard his footsteps retreating along the corridor and down the stairs.

'I think they're next to the kettle!' he said.

Seizing the moment, Imogen opened the door of the study and scampered along the corridor as quickly and quietly as she could, taking extra care as she passed the stairwell. She opened the door of her bedroom, tucked her notebook underneath an old teddy bear and dived into bed. And, after her mind had stopped racing, she fell asleep, feeling very much like a detective.

## Chapter Eight

# Christmas Shopping

Central London was fizzing with Christmas lights.

There was something about school having broken up that made the streets feel bright and sparkling no matter how dull the sky was, like Christmas didn't need to prove itself any more. Imogen kept Einstein in her pocket and had to be dragged away from almost every shop window they walked past – with all the tinsel and fake snow, even supermarkets and unfashionable clothing stores for old men seemed suddenly fascinating.

Arthur was less keen on busy streets. He liked the decorations too, but for Arthur being in a crowd was a little like being underwater. He kept hold of Mrs Stewart's hand and tried to avoid the tourists who weaved about him in directionless lines and paused in difficult places to put up umbrellas. Each time a taxi or bus came whooshing past, the buildings looming overhead would seem suddenly taller and more menacing.

'Here we are,' said Mrs Stewart, steering him left into a great big department store.

They stood still at last to ride the escalator, and Arthur breathed a sigh of relief. As he watched all the baubles floating past in pretty colours, it was finally quiet enough to remember what Imogen was so excited about.

'Imogen!' he said. 'Make sure Einstein gets to see the decorations!'

But Einstein was one step ahead of him, and was

already trying to remove a string of tinsel from the edge of the escalator with his beak.

'Einstein, no!' said Imogen. She leaped to the other side of the escalator so that Einstein could no longer reach it, but rather than forcing him to let go, as she'd hoped, the sudden movement only caused Einstein to tug harder. All at once, the whole string of tinsel from the left-hand side of the escalator broke free from where it was fastened. Imogen, Arthur and Mrs Stewart watched as it tumbled, sparkling red, to land with an echoing flop on the ground floor below.

They looked at each other for a moment, wide-eyed. Then, 'Quick, run!' Mrs Stewart cried, and she started to rush up the remainder of the escalator.

'Where to?' said Arthur, bounding up the steps to keep up with her.

'I don't know! Into a shop!' she said. 'And give me that penguin, Imogen!'

Einstein honked indignantly as Mrs Stewart grabbed him out of Imogen's pocket and shoved him sideways into her handbag.

'We are just a normal family,' Mrs Stewart hissed, taking each of her children by the hand and leading them into the first shop they came across. 'Walking very casually into a men's clothing store.'

Einstein gave a wriggle from inside her handbag, squawked sulkily, poked the fabric once with his flipper and reluctantly settled down.

'Ooh, do you think Dad would like this for Christmas, Imogen?' said Mrs Stewart, raising her voice back to a normal volume as she examined a leather satchel.

'He already has one a bit like that,' said Imogen.

'That's how we know he'd like it . . .' said Mrs Stewart. 'But what about this scarf?'

'I thought we were going to the toyshop,' said Arthur sulkily.

'Not until we've picked out presents for Dad and your grandparents.'

'Maybe they'd like toys too?'

'You'll get toys for Christmas, Arthur,' said Imogen, feeling particularly grown up all of a sudden. 'Stop being such a baby.'

Eventually they settled on a nice new belt for Mr Stewart, and some woolly gloves to send to their grandfather. Imogen hadn't yet found a moment to tell her brother about last night's discovery, and tried to get his attention several times as they walked through the department store towards the toyshop. But Arthur was in a sulk with her, and pretended to be far too interested in his own shoes to notice when she said his name.

'Arthur,' said Imogen, for the third time. 'I have to tell you something.'

'Why would you have to tell me something if I'm only a baby?' said Arthur.

'Well, you *definitely* sound like one now!' said Imogen.

'Stop bickering,' said Mrs Stewart. 'Let's just pop into the food section to get some of those ginger biscuits Granny likes.'

'The food section smells like fish,' Arthur grumbled.

The entrance did smell like fish, but beyond the fish counters were various stalls piled high with cakes and chocolates. Suddenly Imogen and Arthur were far too busy working out how many they could buy with their pocket money to remember they had fallen out. The chocolates were all very expensive, though, and after last week's cupcake purchase Imogen only had 20p left in her pocket. Luckily the man behind the counter let them both have a free sample, and didn't even mind when Imogen said vaguely, 'They're lovely! We might buy some later . . .' and then quickly shuffled off.

'Anyway,' said Imogen, as Arthur stood on his

tiptoes and glanced around to see where Mrs Stewart had got to, 'I think Isaac's in Edinburgh.'

Arthur looked at her. 'Why?'

'I found a news article. They're from Sydney Zoo, both of them. And then Isaac was moved to a zoo somewhere in the UK. The article didn't say which zoo, but Einstein already checked if Isaac was in London. And there's a picture of a rockhopper penguin in Edinburgh that looks exactly like Isaac.'

'What's a rockhopper penguin?'

'The sort of penguin Isaac is.'

'So what do we do?' asked Arthur.

'I don't know,' said Imogen. She bit her lip seriously. 'Maybe we'll have to run away.'

'Why don't we just tell Mum and Dad?'

It had never really occurred to Imogen that she could *tell* her parents something like that, and she considered it for a moment – but of course it still wouldn't work. Mr Stewart had always made it clear that Einstein was only staying until they found out where his real home was.

'If we tell them that Einstein comes from Sydney Zoo, then they'll call the zoo and send him home!' Imogen pointed out, her stomach sinking as she said it. 'People from the zoo are probably already looking for him. Mum will think it's wrong to keep him a secret and then—'

'Imogen! Arthur!'

Suddenly Mrs Stewart appeared beside them with the box of ginger biscuits in her hand. She looked frantic. 'I've lost him!'

'*What?*'

'I noticed when I was getting my purse out! He's gone from my handbag! Einstein!'

'How can he be gone?' said Arthur.

'Do you think they arrested him for breaking the tinsel?' said Imogen.

Then, all at once, everyone remembered.

'Fish!' they cried in unison, and turned to run towards the entrance of the food hall.

Mrs Stewart headed for the door, where the view was best, while Imogen ran towards the fish counters and Arthur, being the smallest, crouched down to look around for penguins hiding at knee height.

'I can't see him!' cried Imogen, pushing past a disgruntled pair of old men who had been asking about some expensive-looking salmon. She glanced desperately up and down the ice-filled glass cases. It was Einstein's idea of heaven: he could be anywhere. But she was met only with the slimy, silvery stare of row upon row of cold, dead fish. Imogen shuddered and turned away.

She looked up at the person standing closest to her. 'Excuse me, have you seen a—'

Imogen froze. It was him: it was the man who had taken her poster down – she was sure of it. He was real, after all, and he was still dressed in his hat and long white coat, and he was peering down at her with great interest.

'A what, love?' he prompted.

Perhaps he *did* know something, but looking up at his face Imogen felt quite certain – with the sort of gut feeling Inspector Bucket liked to work on – that this was not a man she could trust. There was something about the way his eyebrow arched as he looked at her, about the serious lines in his oddly pale face.

'A cat,' she finished faintly.

The man looked surprised. 'No, I haven't seen any cats,' he said.

'Don't worry,' said Imogen, smiling quickly. 'Thank you for your help!' She pushed past him and ran back towards her brother.

'Have you seen him?' said Arthur, standing up from the floor.

'No, have you?' Imogen's heart was pounding. She was still looking out for Einstein, but she couldn't stop glancing over at the man. And she had the horrible feeling that he was watching her back.

'I can't,' said Arthur. 'There's too many people.' It was true: the black and white tiled floor that seemed to stretch endlessly around them was covered in people, and entirely empty of penguins.

'There!' cried Imogen. Across the hall, a woman in

an apron and a funny straw hat was wheeling several crates of fish along behind the counters. Just for a moment, Imogen thought she saw a dark blue flipper poke through one of the gaps.

'Where?' said Arthur.

She glanced over at where the man in the white coat had been standing – good, he had turned round. 'Follow me!'

Imogen led the way as they pushed through the crowd back to the fish counters. 'Excuse me!' she said, as they reached the lady in the straw hat.

The woman paused and looked down at the two small children, who were both panting and looking flustered. 'Yes?'

'I'd like to see your fish, please,' said Imogen, through another pant.

'There's fish on the counters,' said the woman, and started to walk away again.

'No, no, wait!' cried Imogen. 'I'd like to see *your* fish.'

'*My* fish?'

'What I mean is,' said Imogen, 'are you sure that's *fish* in there?'

'Look – do you kids have an adult with you or should I call security?'

'There!' shouted Arthur, tugging on Imogen's sleeve and pointing desperately at the bottom crate. 'I saw his arm!'

'An arm?!' The woman in the funny hat looked horrified, and started to quickly unload the crates from her trolley.

'I mean flipper,' said Arthur.

The woman lifted the second-to-last crate, and up popped Einstein's head.

'Einstein!' cried Imogen.

Einstein squawked sheepishly and let her pick him up. Imogen wiped the fish scales off his feathers with her coat sleeve, patted him on the head and put him back in her pocket.

'Phew,' she said. 'Can you see Mum, Arthur?'

Then they remembered the woman.

She was staring down at them, her eyebrows raised so high that it looked like her straw hat was about to pop off the top of her head. Imogen stared back, and then all three of them turned to the crate they had pulled Einstein out of.

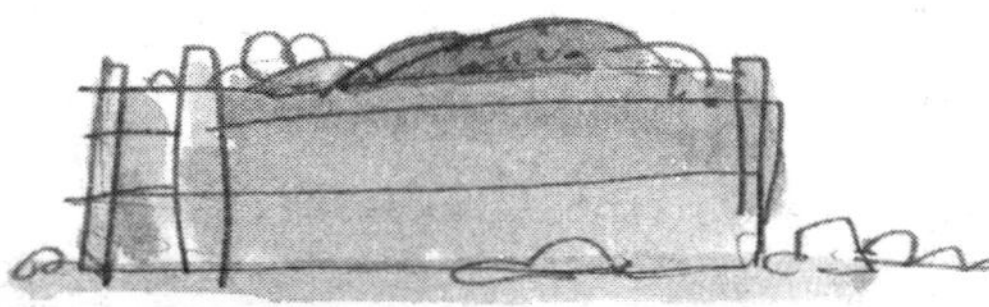

It was a mess. Half the fish were gone, and the rest were pecked to pieces.

'He's gone and eaten all my sardines!' said the woman.

Imogen and Arthur looked at each other.

'We have to go,' said Arthur.

'I should probably call security . . .' said the woman, frowning.

'And we should probably go,' said Imogen, backing away as the woman's disbelief started to turn, very slowly, to anger.

'Will Mum have to pay?' asked Arthur, as they quickly walked towards the door.

'I don't know,' said Imogen, and they broke into a run.

'Mum!'

'Arthur!' Mrs Stewart was still looking around near the entrance. 'Have you found him?'

'He's in my coat,' said Imogen. 'We need to go!'

'Why? What's happened?' asked Mrs Stewart, but she knew not to stick around to find out.

They all hurried over to the escalator. Then, just as Imogen was about to jump on to it, she crashed into someone, who stumbled and dropped the pieces of paper he'd been holding.

'Sorry,' said Imogen, and quickly bent down to pick up his things. 'Hang on,' she frowned. At the top of the pile was a picture of Einstein and Isaac, and underneath that a cutout of the very newspaper article she had discovered last night.

Her cheeks burned red as she looked up, but she already knew whose face she was going to see: it was the same man again. Mrs Stewart and Arthur had disappeared down the escalator. They wouldn't be able to see her, and they wouldn't be able to see him, either.

'Sorry, dear,' the man began, reaching out a hand to take the photos back from her. 'That was my fault

really. I wasn't looking.' He spoke in a mild Australian accent: she hadn't noticed that before.

Imogen took a step backwards, gaping at him like a fish.

'Can I have those back? They're very important.' He came closer, still holding out his hand.

'No!' shouted Imogen, so loudly that even she was surprised by the sound of her own voice, and she darted away from him and hurried down the escalator, following the red streak of colour that was Mrs Stewart's coat – just as it disappeared on to the street outside.

They were hailing a taxi when Imogen caught up with them.

'What about the toyshop?' said Arthur hopefully, as they clambered in. But he didn't really mean it.

Imogen sank down into her seat, avoiding the

window, and she kept her breath held until the taxi had pulled away from the pavement and joined the nameless flood of traffic heading out of central London.

## Chapter Nine

# A Difficult Decision

Imogen turned the man's newspaper cutout over in her hands and looked at it again.

**Lost Penguin's Daring Escape From Sydney Zoo Filmed On CCTV**

Some bullet points were scrawled in black pen in the margin, listing Einstein's flight details. Further down the page, the man seemed to have come to the same conclusion that she had:

She folded it back over and shuddered. It all seemed so sinister all of a sudden. What did the man want with Einstein? What did he want with Isaac? And, if *he* knew Isaac was in Edinburgh, what was to stop him from getting there first? All the sorts of criminals Imogen had read about in her detective books came flooding through her head. Perhaps he was an art thief: she didn't think art thieves had much interest in penguins, but you never could tell with villains. Or maybe a kidnapper? That seemed likely: kidnappers would probably kidnap anyone they could get their hands on, penguin or otherwise.

Even so, she didn't know how to find and rescue Isaac without asking her parents for help and, if she did ask them for help, she'd have to tell them the truth about where Einstein had come from. And then they'd send him home to Sydney. But if she did nothing? Imogen didn't know what would happen if she did nothing, but she had a terrible feeling about it. The sort of feeling that makes your insides go all fidgety.

There was a small knock at her bedroom door.

'Come in!' Imogen said.

It was Arthur. Einstein waddled in after him.

'Mum wants to know if you want anything to eat,' said Arthur.

'I'm not hungry.'

Arthur frowned. 'Are you sure?' he asked. 'You're usually hungry.'

Imogen sat down on her bed. 'Well, I'm not hungry today. I have to think.'

'Are you thinking about your detective work?' asked Arthur.

'I don't know,' said Imogen. 'I'm not sure I want to be a detective any more.'

'But we're so close to finding Isaac!'

Einstein looked up and squawked in interest: now Arthur had given her away.

'I don't know, Einstein,' said Imogen apologetically. 'I think Isaac might be in Edinburgh, but I can't be sure without going there.'

'Have you got the picture of the penguin in Edinburgh?' said Arthur. 'Einstein will be able to tell if it's Isaac or not. Won't you, Einstein?'

Imogen's stomach did another somersault. She wasn't sure Arthur understood their problem, but she wasn't sure she had any other choice, either.

'Okay,' said Imogen. 'Get Mum's laptop and I'll show you the photo.'

Arthur hurried along the corridor and came back with the laptop a moment later. When Imogen opened it up and searched for the photo, Einstein erupted in such an excited flurry of squawks and clucks that Arthur had to slam the door shut to stop their parents from hearing.

'Shh,' said Imogen. 'Don't hit the screen with your flipper!'

Arthur grabbed the laptop off his sister and stared at it. 'Where's Einstein's photo of Isaac?' he asked, and Imogen took her detective notebook out of her dressing-gown pocket, opened it to the right page and handed it to him.

They set the two side by side, and looked from one to the other. It was just as Imogen had thought the night before: hard to tell, of course, but the feathers were the same – and, with Einstein's reaction, it was almost certain . . .

Then, leaning over with her pen, Imogen added to last week's spider diagram:

Isaac is definitely in Edinburgh.

Arthur grinned excitedly. 'So let's tell Mum and Dad. We need to go to Edinburgh and find him!'

Imogen nodded, but she seemed uncertain.

'What's wrong?' asked Arthur.

'If Mum and Dad find out where Einstein's really from, then they'll tell Sydney Zoo. What if he doesn't like living in a zoo?'

Arthur stopped grinning. 'We could leave that bit of the story out?' he suggested hopefully.

'But how can we tell them about Isaac without telling them everything else too? We'll have to show them the newspaper article just to persuade them we're not making it up.'

'Well, maybe we can convince Mum and Dad to let us keep him anyway,' said Arthur.

'Maybe,' Imogen agreed, but she didn't really think so. Even if Mr and Mrs Stewart *wanted* to keep Einstein, there was no way they'd keep the story secret. It wasn't the sort of secret a grown-up would like to keep. Mr Stewart was too honest, and Mrs Stewart would worry too much. And, if Sydney Zoo wanted Einstein back, what was to stop them from taking the penguin that was rightfully theirs?

'And if we *don't* ask them for help . . .' said Arthur.

'Then I only have twenty pee and two paperclips in my moneybox, so we won't go to Edinburgh *or* find Isaac,' Imogen finished. 'And there's something else I haven't told you,' she said. 'I saw someone at the department store,' and she explained all about the strange man, and how he'd taken their poster down, and how he seemed to have followed them. She showed her brother the notes and the photos he had been carrying.

'So what does he want?' asked Arthur.

Imogen shook her head. 'I don't know,' she said. 'But he's clearly looking for Isaac too.'

'Then we have to go!' said Arthur. 'What if he wants to hurt Isaac? We have to stop him!'

Einstein honked.

Imogen nodded. 'I know,' she said. 'But what if

he's in Edinburgh when we get there? And what if he wants to hurt Einstein too?'

'Then we'll fight him!' said Arthur. He thought about Einstein pecking Jack Jones's ears in the changing room at school, and felt suddenly much braver than usual.

Imogen knew that he was right. There wasn't any other choice – and, besides, it seemed fitting that she, a detective, should have an arch-nemesis on her trail. It made her feel important, as well as a little scared.

'You're right. We don't have to tell Mum and Dad that bit about the strange man, though.'

'Why not?'

'Because they might not let us go to Edinburgh if they really think it's dangerous.' She left a dramatic pause, just for effect. 'This is something we need to sort out for ourselves.'

'What do you think, Einstein?' Arthur asked. 'We're a family now, aren't we?'

Einstein looked up sadly from the laptop screen and nodded.

'But he only met us because he was looking for Isaac. That's why he's really here,' said Imogen. 'Squawk once if you want to go to Edinburgh and find Isaac, and twice if you don't.'

There was a long silence. Einstein stared at the laptop screen, and then up at his human friends. Then he gave a long, single squawk.

CHAPTER TEN

# Train to Edinburgh

After they had told their parents everything, Imogen felt ashamed that she had ever been indecisive. After all, she'd always known that Einstein's time with them was temporary. She had just convinced herself that they might be able to keep him forever. But he wasn't like one of her toys, was he? He was a real penguin, with real penguin friends and a real penguin family, even if they were from a zoo. All she had done was make everything harder for herself – and for Arthur too.

Still, she couldn't help but feel nervous about it. The strange man's notes had *said* Edinburgh on them. She kept imagining walking up to the zoo and finding him waiting there with a net, ready to steal Einstein away from her.

'Cheer up, Im!' said Mr Stewart, as he shoved their overnight bags into the back of the taxi. 'We're going on an adventure!'

Of course, her father couldn't possibly understand the seriousness of the situation. As far as Imogen could tell, Mr Stewart was viewing their trip to Edinburgh as some sort of holiday. She sighed crossly and brushed her hair out of her face. She would have to be the responsible one yet again: grown-ups never understood anything.

'I don't know what you're so happy about, James,' said Mrs Stewart. All day at home she had hardly been able to sit down for five minutes without springing up to check the answer machine or peer anxiously out of the window.

'Neither do I,' said Mr Stewart amusedly. 'Although I suppose now that we're going to Edinburgh, we might stop the police from finding us and pressing charges for damaged tinsel?'

'James, that is *not* funny!'

Mr Stewart chuckled and sat down beside her in the back of the taxi. Arthur and Imogen took the two fold-down seats that faced the back. It was late evening, and they both looked tired. Arthur snuggled Einstein close to his chest and fell into a light doze as the taxi started to move.

The driver eyed Einstein suspiciously through the rear-view mirror. 'They make them very realistic these days, don't they?' he said.

Mrs Stewart laughed awkwardly and said something about the weather.

'Anyway,' she went on, 'if the children are right about Einstein being from Sydney Zoo, imagine what will happen if someone who recognises him sees yesterday's CCTV footage from the department store?'

Imogen thought about the man again. Had he seen the footage? Did he know Einstein was with them, or did he only suspect it?

'I don't know,' said Mr Stewart blankly. 'What *will* happen?'

'Well, I think the whole thing's a bit far-fetched,' Mrs Stewart sniffed. 'I don't know why we're humouring Imogen's conspiracy theories.'

'I am a professional detective!' Imogen protested, but she was only half listening, and quickly went back to watching two pigeons on the street outside fighting over a soggy-looking crisp.

Mr Stewart shrugged. 'The whole thing was pretty ridiculous in the first place, though, wasn't it? No harm in accepting a bit *more* ridiculousness now that we've started.'

'If we all accepted that as a principle, then the

whole world would have gone mad years ago!'

'You're the one who's been cooking gourmet meals for a penguin, dear.'

Mrs Stewart sniffed again and checked her watch. 'The last train to Edinburgh leaves in twenty minutes,' she said. 'Let's hope the traffic's good.'

They had meant to leave with more time to spare, but getting everyone out of the house was always challenging. As soon as one person had found their shoes, someone else would have lost theirs, and then the cat would want feeding and the bathroom door would get stuck, and then all of a sudden it was past ten o'clock and the sleeper train's departure time was approaching fast.

On top of that, Mr and Mrs Stewart kept bickering and changing their minds.

'He's officially a missing penguin,' Mr Stewart had said, after seeing Imogen's newspaper article. 'We can't just take him to Edinburgh! We need to report this straight away.'

'Oh, but how would you feel if *you* were all alone in a strange place, looking for a long-lost friend?' Mrs Stewart had retorted. 'Would *you* want to be packed off home?'

Then, every few minutes, they would swap. 'I just don't know if we should be doing this . . .' Mrs Stewart would mutter under her breath. And all of a sudden everyone was arguing again.

'Stop it!' Arthur had shouted eventually. It was usually Imogen who did the shouting, so the shock of it made them all fall silent. 'Einstein has come all the way across the world to find his friend! Are you really going to stop him at the last minute just because you can't stop arguing?'

Einstein followed this with a loud squawk, for good measure.

'No, you're right . . .' Mr Stewart muttered awkwardly. 'I'd better phone a taxi.'

The taxi got caught in several traffic lights near the station. Mr Stewart couldn't stop checking his watch and peering anxiously out of the window. Eventually he got fed up.

'Don't worry about parking, we'll get out here,' he told the driver, and handed the money over with a tip.

Of course, he was only worried about losing money on the train tickets, Imogen thought to herself. But she was glad to see him hurry all the same.

'Why aren't we parking?' asked Arthur sleepily.

'We're going to have to run for it.'

Mr and Mrs Stewart jumped out and grabbed the bags from the back, and Imogen and Arthur followed them out on to the dark, drizzling street. Imogen was starting to feel very sleepy too. When her father shouted, 'Let's go!' and everyone rushed towards the station, she felt a bit like she was running in her sleep.

It was late, so the platform was mostly empty. Mrs Stewart quickly checked the departures board and they ran towards the waiting train, which was just about ready to leave. One of the conductors on the platform tutted as Mr Stewart slammed the button to open the carriage.

‘Ten seconds later and you’d have missed it!’ he said.

Imogen and Mrs Stewart jumped on to the train, and Mr Stewart turned round to wait for Arthur, who was just behind them. Keeping hold of Einstein had slowed him down a little.

‘Come on,’ said Mr Stewart, reaching out his hand.

Suddenly Arthur froze.

‘Come *on*!’ said Mr Stewart.

‘That doesn’t say Edinburgh!’ said Arthur, staring up at the screen beside the train. The lenses of his glasses were spattered with raindrops, and he wasn’t quite sure how to spell ‘Edinburgh’ anyway, but he was sure it wasn’t spelled like *that*. ‘You’re on the wrong train!’

Mr Stewart’s eyes widened as he saw what the screen said too. ‘Imogen! Rachel! Get off the train! This one’s going to Liverpool!’

They jumped back down to the platform just as the

train doors hissed to a close behind them.

'Which one is it?!' cried Imogen.

'Edinburgh's platform six, not nine,' said the same conductor who had tutted at them a moment earlier. He checked his watch. 'You won't make it.'

Mrs Stewart grabbed hold of Einstein, Mr Stewart picked up Arthur, and everyone ran as fast as they possibly could to platform six. Imogen was pretty sure no other nine-year-old had run so quickly before, and that, if only Mr Burnett had seen her, she'd have been made captain of every team in school.

They jumped on to the train with seconds to spare.

It took a while to find the right compartment. Mr Stewart had made everyone jump into the first carriage they could reach, but the one with their rooms in was all the way at the front of the train. They walked down the narrow corridors as the train started to rumble and move beneath them, slowly winding its way out of London.

It was a biggish compartment, with two bunk beds at either end. Imogen had secretly imagined something grander: she'd never been on a sleeper train before, and thought of them as being like trains from the olden days, with polished wood and chandeliers, whereas this one looked quite modern and ordinary. Arthur didn't mind, though. He was too busy claiming the top bunk for himself and Einstein.

'I get the top bunk, remember?' said Imogen.

Arthur looked blank. 'But I got here first,' he said.

Imogen raised an eyebrow at him, and suddenly he remembered.

'But that only applies to cars!' said Arthur, in protest.

'*Dad!*' Imogen started. 'Guess what Arthur did last—'

'Okay, fine!' said Arthur, and he hopped back down, looking sulky.

'Straight to sleep,' said Mrs Stewart. 'When you

wake up, we'll be in Edinburgh!'

Although she was tired, Imogen didn't drift off straight away. She lay still in the top bunk, watching light move through the chink in the blinds, and listening to her parents whispering on the other side of the compartment. Sometimes the light would shine through two chinks at once and she thought it looked like dragon eyes blinking at her.

Arthur gave Einstein his second pillow, and made sure to lend him a corner of duvet too. Soon they left London behind, and the light stopped flickering in quite so often. And so they fell asleep to the gentle rumbling of the train tracks, and the pattering of rain against the roof.

## Chapter Eleven

# Detective Bill Hunter

It was hardly morning when the train pulled into Edinburgh Waverley Station.

They had been woken up half an hour beforehand by a loud lady with a trolley of breakfast things. Arthur was far too excited to mind that it was early, and quickly sprang to life.

'Is that a dog?' said the trolley-lady, catching a glimpse of Einstein beneath the covers as Arthur threw back his duvet.

Arthur went pink. 'Oh – er . . .'

'It's all right,' said the lady. 'They're allowed. Just keep him out of the bed, all right?'

Arthur nodded quickly.

Imogen felt it was far too early to be very hungry, and could only nibble on the corner of a dry-tasting shortbread. 'I don't like it,' she said eventually, and handed the rest to Arthur, who ate ten.

Mr Stewart sipped some black coffee while Mrs Stewart scrolled on her phone. 'Looks like the zoo won't be open yet,' she said. 'But we can go somewhere nice for breakfast first. If Arthur still has any room for breakfast, that is.'

It was a bright grey sort of day in Edinburgh. The sun started to rise shortly after they'd left the station, though you wouldn't have noticed if it wasn't for the fading darkness: the sky was one great cloud, without a gap in it to let a sunbeam through. Still, Arthur thought it suited the grey stone walls of the old buildings, and made the castle up on the hill look like something out of a storybook.

They found a café to sit down in for breakfast. Imogen had woken up enough to regain her appetite, and ate most of a stack of pancakes. Arthur, still full of shortbread, nibbled at the edges of the few she left, while Mr and Mrs Stewart had boring grown-up things like yoghurt and fruit.

'Do you have any raw herrings?' Mrs Stewart asked the waitress, when she came over to check that everything was all right.

The waitress looked confused. 'Is this for you?'

'Oh, no,' Mrs Stewart laughed bashfully. 'Just for the penguin, of course!'

The waitress spotted Einstein sitting between the two children on the far side of the table and jumped. 'Oh!' she said, and shook her head slightly, as if to check she was really awake. 'No . . . we don't have much call for raw herrings. But I could do kippers?'

'Ooh, could you do them with marmalade?' said Mrs Stewart. '*What*, James? He *likes* marmalade!'

'Sure,' said the waitress, and she wandered back to the kitchen in a daze.

Einstein gobbled up the first half of his plate of kippers in high spirits, but slowed down over the rest. Eventually he stopped eating altogether.

'Oh, dear,' said Mr Stewart dryly. 'Maybe he doesn't like the marmalade, after all.'

'He's just nervous,' Imogen explained.

She knew how he felt. Now that she'd finished her pancakes, she was feeling a little queasy too. What if Isaac wasn't there, after all, or that man had got to him first? And, even if Isaac was there, what would they do with him? They couldn't just steal him away from the zoo, could they? And she didn't suppose there was much chance of Edinburgh Zoo agreeing to send Isaac back to Sydney. They'd come such a long way just to see a penguin through the walls of an enclosure. Maybe their adventure would turn out to be a disappointing one.

'Are you okay?' Arthur asked his sister a little later as they wandered past the flamingoes on the way into the zoo.

'Of course,' said Imogen, and she gave him her reassuring smile.

Arthur was feeling pretty happy himself, but it made him nervous when Imogen went quiet. He was only her assistant, after all: she was the one who tended to notice things first. So, when she wore her thoughtful face, he worried that he had missed something obvious, like when he hadn't been able to see that Einstein's stay might be cut short by all this detective work. But he was trying not to think about that.

The zoo had only just opened, so it was still quiet, and they had a good view of all the animals they walked past. Mr Stewart made everyone stop at the flamingoes, and again at the red pandas, and again at the monkeys, until eventually Mrs Stewart got tired.

'Can we get on with seeing the penguins?' she said, rolling her eyes.

'The children like the monkeys,' said Mr Stewart defensively. 'No need to get impatient.' But he hurried up all the same.

As they turned the corner towards the penguin enclosure, Imogen's nervousness quickly turned to excitement. Einstein was tucked safely inside her coat. Arthur had wanted to keep Einstein inside

his own coat, but it was much smaller, so Einstein's flippers were in danger of poking out and giving them away.

'Remember, look for the ones with the spiky yellow eyebrows,' said Imogen, as she and Arthur started to run ahead of their parents.

'There's so many of them!' said Arthur.

The penguin enclosure was large. A great big lake stretched across it, with artificial beaches round the edges that sloped down into the water. Imogen and Arthur started by running over the bridge that went across the middle. There were penguins swimming

in the water underneath them, and more waddling about on the tarmac banks, but none of them looked like Isaac.

Arthur frowned and pulled himself up on the railings to get a better view. 'There!' he said.

'What?' said Imogen. 'I don't see anything!'

'On the far side of the lake! I thought I saw some with yellow eyebrows!'

He led the way. They ran across the bridge and followed a ramp down the side of the lake until they reached a small platform with glass walls that formed a window into the middle of the water. When Arthur stood on it, penguins swam past him at head height. The water was murky blue, and the birds appeared like shadows against it. He peered through the glass and tried to spot the penguin he had seen a moment ago.

'That was the one I saw,' said Arthur uncertainly.

'That's not Isaac,' said Imogen, but Arthur already

knew. This penguin's eyebrows were more white than yellow, and anyway it was too big.

Arthur sighed and traipsed back towards the top of the lake. Imogen followed. She couldn't see Isaac anywhere: she couldn't even see any rockhopper penguins. This was exactly what she had been so afraid of.

'*There* you are!' said Mrs Stewart, as their parents finally caught up with them.

Mr Stewart huffed and puffed and looked put out at having to hurry.

'We can't find him,' said Imogen, in a very small voice. 'We've looked everywhere.'

'Oh, no,' said Mrs Stewart. 'Perhaps you were wrong, after all?'

'I was *not* wrong,' said Imogen crossly.

'Well, I'm sure Einstein has *other* friends back in Sydney.' Mrs Stewart crouched down and smiled at her, like she used to when Imogen was little and had been upset about something. 'So it's not the end of the world now, is it? We've still had lots of fun!'

Imogen was furious. How could her mother talk to her like that? She wasn't little, and she certainly wasn't upset – she was righteously angry. To suggest that it didn't matter that Isaac was still missing – the very idea was ridiculous!

'We did not come here,' she said through gritted teeth, 'to have *fun*!'

Mr Stewart disguised a chuckle with a fit of coughing. Then, as Imogen looked up to scold him, she saw something moving through the crowd beyond her father's shoulder: a hat, a hat with a very wide brim, and a man in a white coat attached to the bottom of it. He was passing a small building that looked like it might have offices inside, just beyond the penguin enclosure. Imogen squinted. He was about to walk inside, passing under a sign that said **Education Centre**.

'It's him!' she shouted. 'He must have Isaac!'

'It's who, dear?' said Mrs Stewart.

Imogen ignored her. 'Arthur, follow me,' she commanded.

'Imogen, Arthur! Where are you going?! Come back here!' Their mother's voice faded into the crowd as they hurried away from her.

'Excuse me!' said Imogen, in a loud and important sort of voice. 'Excuse me, sir!'

Arthur caught up with her just as the man in the white coat turned to see who was speaking to him. His face darkened. 'You,' he said.

Imogen gaped up at him, and whatever she was about to say got caught somewhere in the middle of her throat. She'd forgotten how scary he looked, with a pale, cross-looking face, and scraggly grey eyebrows that were much too big for his forehead.

'You stole my notes,' he said.

Instinctively Arthur put his hand on Imogen's

elbow, and she puffed her chest out in a renewed bout of bravery. 'And *you* stole my poster,' she retorted.

'I think we need to have a little chat,' said the man.

'So do I!' said Imogen. 'I'd like to ask you some questions!'

The man looked a little confused. 'Right, well.' He glanced around, then pointed to the nearest door. 'In here,' he said. 'After you.'

'No, after you.' Imogen folded her arms.

The man narrowed his eyes and then shrugged. 'Whichever you prefer,' he said. 'I'll be asking you the same questions either way.'

They marched into the room in a sort of procession. Einstein was still tucked safely inside Imogen's coat – she had hissed at him to stay there – and she could feel him start to wriggle impatiently.

It appeared to be some sort of cleaning cupboard. There was an old table in the centre of the room with a couple of rickety-looking chairs pulled up to it. Beyond them were several shelves of cleaning products and a disorganised selection of mops and brooms. The ceiling light was broken, occasionally giving a nervous sputter of electricity, and the blinds were pulled down.

'Sit down,' said Imogen.

The man sat down without thinking, then frowned and jumped back up again. 'Hang on,' he said, and readjusted his hat. 'Detective Bill Hunter,' he announced proudly. 'I'm looking for a penguin, and I think you might be able to help me. Perhaps you could start by telling me your name?'

'What are you doing?' Arthur whispered nervously, but Imogen hushed him.

'DCI Imogen Stewart,' she replied. 'This is my assistant, Arthur. And it just so happens that we're looking for a penguin too.' She wasn't sure what DCI stood for, but she had heard detectives say it like that on the television.

'Right,' said the man, blinking at her. 'You're a – how old are you?'

'Nine and three-quarters.'

Detective Bill Hunter shook his head. 'How can you possibly have reached that rank?'

'I'm not sure that's important right now,' said Imogen, folding her arms.

'No – I suppose not.'

'My poster,' said Imogen. 'Why did you take it down?'

'It was imperative to the operation. I believed that I recognised the penguin in question,' said Bill Hunter. 'Why did you put it up?'

'I was looking for the penguin in question.'

'Why?'

'Because the penguin in question was friends with a different penguin.' Imogen frowned: she had confused herself. 'A penguin in a different question,' she added, though she couldn't quite remember what the question was.

'Einstein,' said Detective Bill Hunter.

Arthur gaped at him, but Imogen kept her face deliberately blank. 'How do you know about Einstein?' she asked.

'How do *you* know about Einstein?' he shot back.

'I'm sorry,' said Imogen sarcastically. 'Who's doing the questioning here?'

'Well, I am.' Bill Hunter frowned. 'Aren't I?'

Now it was Imogen's turn to frown. 'No I am,' she said. She glanced uncertainly over at her brother.

Arthur looked at her significantly. He was thinking back to when Einstein had attacked Jack Jones in the changing rooms at school, but he was much too nervous to say anything, so tried to express the thought to her in glances.

'What?' said Imogen. She turned back to the man. 'Look, are you going to tell us where Isaac is or not?'

'No,' said Bill Hunter. He smiled menacingly. '*You*'re going to tell *me* where Einstein is, or else you'll be very, very sorry.'

'Let him out,' whispered Arthur.

Imogen's stomach did a little somersault. Detective Bill Hunter was towering above her: his hat almost blocked out the flickering ceiling light.

'Let him out of your coat,' said Arthur, more loudly this time.

Imogen did as her brother told her. She undid the top two toggles on her duffel coat and Einstein leaped out from his hiding place like a ball being launched from a very small cannon.

'Aha!' said Detective Bill Hunter triumphantly, and then, a little less triumphantly, 'Ah . . .' He took a step backwards as Einstein jumped at him, and stumbled over as he crashed into the back of one of the rickety chairs, which broke underneath his lumbering weight. He landed on the floor in a heap of wood and chair legs. His hat landed a metre or so away, revealing a mop of wiry grey hair.

'Now stop it—' he began, but he couldn't finish his sentence: Einstein was pecking his ears and tugging his hair with his beak.

Imogen took a step forward. Now *she* was towering over Detective Bill Hunter. 'Where is Isaac?' she asked.

'Get the penguin off me!'

'Have you kidnapped him? Have you murdered him?' Her eyes widened. 'Have you stuffed him and put him in a museum?'

Bill Hunter frowned. 'No, of course not, I – ow! I'm not after Isaac!'

'Einstein, wait,' said Imogen, and Einstein paused his pecking. She took another step forward. 'Who are you after, then?'

'Einstein,' said Bill Hunter. 'I've been employed by Sydney Zoo. I've traced him all the way from Australia.'

'Oh,' said Imogen awkwardly. 'And what are you going to do with him?'

'Well, I was *going* to take him home,' he said,

shooting Einstein a dirty look. 'But now I'm not sure I want to.'

'No, that's fair,' Imogen admitted. 'And . . . Isaac?'

Detective Bill Hunter shrugged. 'I knew Einstein would be looking for him.'

'We're just trying to reunite them,' Arthur piped up. 'Einstein misses his friend – he wanted to make sure he was okay. That's all. We're sorry for causing you trouble.'

Bill Hunter gave a scoffing laugh. 'I don't care what Einstein wants. Doesn't make a difference to my pay cheque.'

Imogen narrowed her eyes at him. 'You need to tell us where Isaac is so that Einstein can see him.'

'Please,' added Arthur.

'I don't and I won't!'

'Einstein, peck him!'

'All right, all right,' said Bill Hunter, shielding his face with his hands. 'He's on the other side of the path.

There's a smaller enclosure with just a few rockhopper penguins inside. Can I get my hat back?'

'You're not going to follow us, are you?' said Imogen.

Then Einstein gave a squawk, and everyone turned to look at him. He had waddled over to one of the cleaning shelves, and was attempting to pick up a roll of masking tape with his beak.

'Now look here,' Bill Hunter began. 'That really won't be necessary—'

'But we're not taking any risks,' Imogen finished,

and Einstein pecked him still while Imogen and Arthur tied him to the chair with masking tape. Then Arthur picked up a mop bucket and placed it upside down over Detective Bill Hunter's head, for good measure.

They looked at each other and smiled.

'Penguin enclosure?' said Imogen.

She scooped Einstein up off the floor and tucked him back into her coat, and Arthur followed her out of the room.

# Chapter Twelve

# Isaac

Mr and Mrs Stewart were still waiting by the penguin enclosure when Imogen and Arthur found them. Mrs Stewart looked frantic.

'Where *have* you two been?' she said.

'Sorry,' said Imogen. They had been gone almost fifteen minutes. 'We were just investigating.'

'We know where Isaac is!' said Arthur.

Mrs Stewart's eyes flashed in anger. 'I should certainly hope you do, young man,' she said, 'after that little performance.'

'We're really very sorry,' said Imogen, 'but it was imperative to the operation.'

'It was what? Since when did you know what "imperative" means?'

Imogen shrugged.

'Your mother's right,' said Mr Stewart. 'You should never run off like that. No matter how upset you are.'

'Sorry,' said Arthur.

'It won't happen again,' Imogen added.

'So where *is* this penguin of yours?'

They led their parents over to the smaller penguin enclosure. Just as Detective Bill Hunter had said, there were the rockhopper penguins. Each one had red eyes surrounded by tufts of yellow feathers, and they were happily splashing around in the water.

'Is that him?' cried Arthur. They pushed their way to the front of the enclosure to get a better look.

'I think he's the one on the right,' said Imogen. She unbuttoned her coat slightly, to give Einstein room to

poke his head out. 'Einstein, can you see your friend?' she asked.

A barely suppressed squawk of happiness from Einstein confirmed what they already knew, but Isaac was oblivious: he couldn't see Einstein yet, and was busy watching a pigeon flap past above his head.

Imogen turned to her parents. 'He's here!' she said. 'He's the one by the rock.'

Mrs Stewart squinted. 'I don't know how you kids can tell the difference . . .' she said vaguely.

'It's Einstein!' said Imogen. 'Look at him! *He* knows!'

'Well, what now?' asked Mr Stewart.

It was a pertinent question. Arthur looked up at his sister.

'I don't know,' said Imogen. She had worried about this earlier: they had found Isaac – Einstein could see him – but what could they do about it? It was a zoo, after all, and enclosures had walls.

'You could hold Einstein up in the air and see if Isaac spots him?' suggested Mrs Stewart, filling in the silence. 'He might come over then.'

'We can't just reveal Einstein in the middle of the zoo,' said Imogen, looking at her mother as if she was an idiot. 'We'll draw attention to ourselves. They'll think we've stolen him.'

'Well, what *can* we do, then?' said Mrs Stewart, a little hurt. 'At least I'm thinking of ideas. You're all thinking of nothing but problems.'

Mr Stewart didn't appear to be thinking of problems, though. In fact, it wasn't clear *what* Mr Stewart was thinking about – only that he was thinking. His hands were in the pockets of his long coat and he was staring out into the penguin enclosure, frowning seriously. Suddenly he strode over to one of the zookeepers, adjusting his tie and straightening his collar as he walked.

'Government zoo inspection,' he said importantly. 'I'd like to take a look at one of your rockhopper penguins.'

Imogen and Arthur gaped at him.

The zookeeper looked startled. 'Oh – sorry, sir. I didn't realise we had an inspection today.'

'Your lack of organisation is none of my concern,' said Mr Stewart, checking his watch pointedly. 'But never mind. Shall we get on?'

'Erm . . . if you come into the office first, we can fill out the paperwork?'

'I'm running late for my next appointment. If we

could do it electronically afterwards, that would be fantastic.'

'I don't think we do electronic forms,' said the zookeeper, baffled.

Mr Stewart raised an eyebrow. 'Really? The system was updated three weeks ago. I'm amazed you haven't caught up with it.'

'Of course, sir. Sorry, sir,' said the zookeeper quickly. 'Which penguin was it you wanted to see?' He opened up a gate in the fence of the enclosure.

'The one by the rock,' Imogen hissed as Mr Stewart walked past.

They waited in the cold for several minutes.

'What do you think he's going to do now?' asked Arthur.

Mrs Stewart shrugged and shook her head. 'The trouble we could get into . . .' she muttered. She still wasn't over Einstein's department-store incident, and seemed twitchier than ever.

Einstein gave an anxious little squawk.

'He's right,' said Imogen, patting Einstein on the head. 'We should follow them.' Mr Stewart and the zookeeper had carried Isaac off round the corner, back towards the Education Centre.

Imogen led the way. She was just fast enough to see the back of her father's leg disappearing into an office. 'Let's listen at the window!' she said.

Arthur hurried after her, while Mrs Stewart – nervous about attracting attention – stuck to the path and strolled up and down it in an attempt to 'look natural'.

'Lucky they didn't go into the storage cupboard . . .' said Arthur.

They crouched down in the flowerbed beneath the office window and Imogen peeked through the blind.

'What's he *doing*?' she whispered.

As her eyes adjusted to the light, she saw Isaac standing on the desk, while a baffled-looking zookeeper watched an equally baffled-looking Mr Stewart measure his flippers with a ruler.

'Right,' said Mr Stewart. 'We'll have him back by three.'

'I'm sorry?' said the zookeeper.

Their voices were muffled through the glass, but Imogen and Arthur could just about strain to hear them.

'He's just making it up,' said Imogen.

'An Australian method,' said Mr Stewart confidently. 'We like to take the penguins out for tea once in a while, see how they're doing. Isaac's from Australia, isn't he?'

'Well, yes,' said the zookeeper. 'He came here to keep one of our other rockhoppers company. How did you know?'

'Jolly good,' said Mr Stewart, scooping Isaac up under one arm and marching purposefully towards the door while the zookeeper was still too confused to stop him.

They met on the steps outside the zoo and quickly hurried down to the pavement, where bushes shaded them from the view of the windows. Mr Stewart wiped his brow with his handkerchief and put Isaac down on the ground.

'*James!*' said Mrs Stewart, half disapproving and half impressed; and, as she didn't know which response she was going for, she was unable to follow it with anything.

Suddenly Isaac let out a gigantic honk. He stared up at Imogen's coat, where Einstein had poked his head through a gap in the buttons.

Einstein honked back.

'Oh, no,' said Mr Stewart, glancing nervously back at the zoo. 'We'd better not do this here.'

But it was too late: Imogen had placed Einstein down on the ground, and Isaac – still letting out the occasional squawk – was bouncing up and down in circles, hopping away in a state of distraction, and then hopping quickly back again to nuzzle his beak against Einstein's.

Arthur grinned, and looked ready to jump up and down too.

'Let's hail this taxi,' said Mrs Stewart, also keen to herd everyone away from the zoo.

'Can we keep Isaac as well?' said Arthur.

'I told the zookeeper I'd have him back by three,' said Mr Stewart firmly. 'But that gives us plenty of time for tea. Shall we go to the Balmoral?'

The Balmoral Hotel was very grand. Imogen thought that, from the outside, it looked like a castle or a sort of palace – somewhere that the Queen might live. The inside had chandeliers hanging from the ceiling and great big armchairs at each of the tables instead of chairs.

No one seemed to consider that they should probably have been eating lunch: it was the sort of event that called for celebration. And that meant tea and cake and scones. Arthur had a hot chocolate, but Imogen was feeling all grown up again, and insisted on sharing her parents' pot of tea. She didn't much like the tea. It was bitter, and tasted nothing like she thought it would. Mr Stewart laughed at her and filled her cup with sugar until it was drinkable.

Isaac and Einstein had an armchair too. The waiter raised an eyebrow when he saw them and whispered something to his manager, but after Mr Stewart went over and spoke to them no one seemed to say another word about it. Imogen thought Einstein looked just like royalty as he pecked at the edge of a carrot cake, and slurped up the puddle of sugary tea she had spilled on to her saucer. Isaac didn't drink any tea, but he had most of one of the pots of jam and got half of it all over the white tablecloth.

Eventually Arthur said what they had all been thinking. 'So Einstein and Isaac won't get to stay together,' he said, 'after Einstein came all this way?'

Imogen scowled at him. 'You'll upset them,' she hissed, but Einstein looked all right. The penguins had been squawking away at each other the whole way in the taxi, and Arthur had listened very hard to see if he could understand them, but whatever penguins spoke wasn't anything like English.

'Well,' said Mrs Stewart, 'he knows *where* Isaac is and that he's happy, and that's the important thing. He doesn't have to worry any more.'

'Yes,' said Mr Stewart. 'The zookeeper said he was settling in well. Led a penguin parade last week, apparently.'

Arthur liked that idea. He imagined Isaac playing the bagpipes as he headed a sort of march round the city. 'So Isaac doesn't mind living in a zoo?'

Mr Stewart looked surprised. 'Why would he mind it? He's always lived in a zoo, hasn't he? I just wonder why Sydney Zoo didn't put more effort into finding Einstein . . .'

Imogen and Arthur glanced at each other.

'You know we'll have to tell Sydney Zoo about Einstein now, don't you?' said Mrs Stewart. 'We can't keep him hidden at home forever. It wouldn't be right.'

'Yes, we knew that. It's just . . .' Imogen began. 'Aren't animals supposed to be free?'

'I suppose so,' said Mr Stewart. 'But, then again, they're not supposed to live in houses in London, either. And *we* don't exactly have a lake for them to swim in.'

'But maybe if we explain everything to the zoos,' said Arthur hopefully, 'they'll let Isaac and Einstein reunite properly?'

'Well, where there's a will there's a way,' said Mr Stewart. 'I can help you write the letter.'

'And maybe Einstein can visit us again?' added Arthur.

'He'll certainly have an open invite,' said Mrs Stewart.

Arthur supposed that that would have to do for now.

After tea, Mrs Stewart suggested a walk round the city. Arthur didn't usually like walks with the family: they were cold and boring, and his parents never understood when he wanted to stop and examine something.

But walking round Edinburgh with two penguins was completely different. It seemed like the other pedestrians hadn't seen many penguins about, and lots of them stopped and stared, or poked each other and whispered in surprise.

Still, neither Einstein nor Isaac minded the attention, and they fluffed up their feathers with pride. Imogen didn't mind it, either, and wandered around with her head held high, as if she went for walks with penguins every day, and disapproved of anyone who didn't. The grey sky was turning white at the edges and, in the little sunlight that shone through the clouds, she felt quite sure that it was sparkling.

Even the ground beneath her feet felt different: it was firmer than usual, and somehow bouncy. The wind felt sharp and bright and the pavements smelled of rain getting ready to fall. She was a detective. She had solved her first case. And Isaac and Einstein walking side by side just a few metres away – that was all because of her.

When it was time to drop Isaac back at the zoo, everyone was exhausted.

Imogen and Arthur both hugged him goodbye, Einstein gave him a beak-nuzzle, and Mrs Stewart leaned down to say, 'Now, dear,' and used her handkerchief to wipe a lump of jam off his feathers.

'Are we ready, then?' said Mr Stewart, and he led Isaac back up the steps towards the ticket office, straightening his collar as he went.

## CHAPTER THIRTEEN

# Christmas

Arthur woke up early on Christmas Day, too early to go downstairs, so he looked out of his bedroom window and watched the sunrise. Grey clouds were heaving themselves awake and slouching about in the sky above the city, occasionally stopping to shimmer in a half-hearted patch of light. Down below, a pigeon was rummaging through the dustbins in the street and a pair of robins were hopping in and out of a hedge.

Just as he was wondering whether it was still too early to wake his sister, the door creaked open.

'Arthur!'

It was Imogen. She had pulled last year's Christmas jumper on over the top of her blue pyjamas, and failed to brush her hair. 'Let's go downstairs – it's Einstein's last day!'

'*And* it's Christmas,' Arthur reminded her, but this seemed somehow secondary. Arthur had spent hours and hours on Christmas Eve putting Einstein's present together, and it was that thought, more than anything, that had woken him up so early.

He followed his sister down the stairs. Somewhere behind their parents' bedroom door Mr Stewart groaned at the sound of creaking floorboards, and Imogen giggled and looked guilty.

Einstein was awake already too. Mr and Mrs

Stewart hadn't been sure, upon questioning, whether penguins celebrated Christmas, but, seeing Einstein waiting for them on the sofa downstairs, Imogen felt quite certain that they did.

'Merry Christmas, Einstein!' she cried, and dug her hand into the box of decorations to find him a Santa hat. She picked out Arthur's hat from a couple of years ago, which was much too big for Einstein's head, but when Imogen tied it back with a piece of tinsel she could just about get it to stay on. Then, in a fit of inspiration, she decided it might be nice if they woke their parents up with coffee, and had broken a mug before a minute was out.

'Do you know how to make coffee?' asked Arthur, who wanted to watch TV.

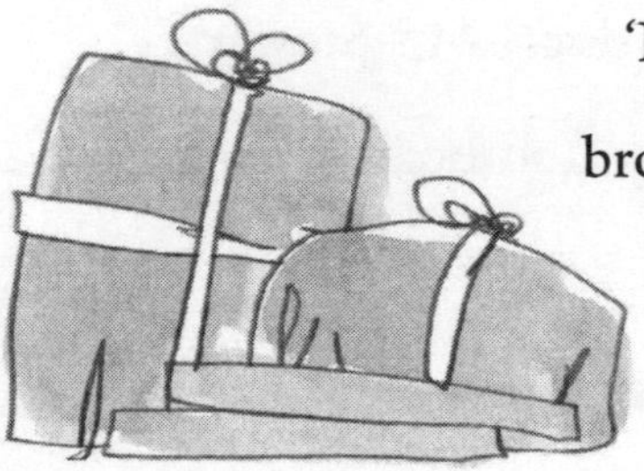

'No,' said Imogen, sweeping the broken pieces of china in the general direction of the bin. 'But I think you use coffee powder.'

She found some on the shelf and read the label while the kettle boiled. 'How many spoons do you think I should use?'

Arthur shrugged. 'Four?' he guessed.

Imogen nodded seriously. 'Maybe a few more,' she said. 'Just in case.'

She balanced the coffee very carefully on the way up the stairs, only spilling a tiny bit on to the tray. *This is going to be a very good Christmas,* she thought to herself, as she pushed open the door of her parents' bedroom.

'Merry Christmas! I brought you your coffee.'

Mr Stewart sat up in bed and rubbed his eyes. 'What time is it?'

'It's past eight,' said Imogen.

Mrs Stewart was impressed. 'Wow, well done!' she said. 'I didn't know you could make coffee.'

'Neither did I!' Imogen grinned, and Mr Stewart looked trepidatious.

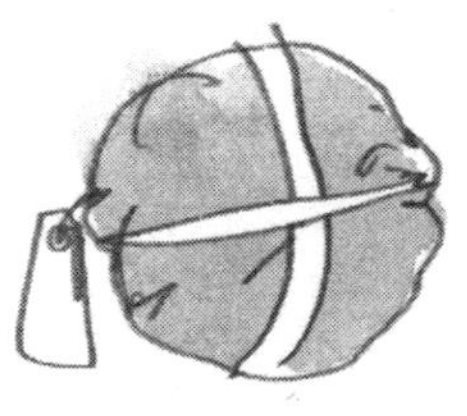

All in all, Imogen was pleased

with the coffee's reception. It was just a *bit* strong, Mr Stewart had said, but not bad for a first go. Neither of them finished their cups, but then again they often didn't. Mrs Stewart placed them both back on the tray and got up to look for her dressing gown.

'It's Einstein's last day . . .' said Imogen a little sadly, though of course her parents already knew that. Mr Stewart had called Sydney Zoo as soon as they returned from Edinburgh, and the woman he spoke to on the phone had been so surprised by the story that she had quickly agreed to let Einstein stay the extra few days until Christmas.

'How funny! We sent a detective out to look for him ourselves, but we haven't heard a peep,' she had said, and then laughed. 'We'll have someone collect him from Heathrow on Boxing Day. And perhaps we'll send a few reporters too!'

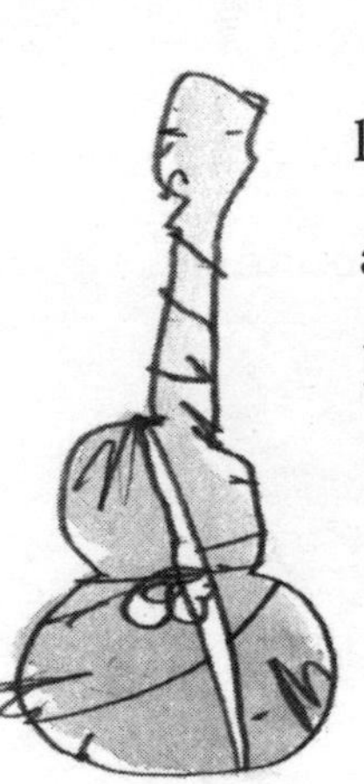

Imogen liked that second idea. Maybe

Einstein would make the newspapers again and, if he did, surely *she* would too, and she'd become a world-renowned detective, and people would travel from far and wide to speak to her, and Einstein would visit every Christmas forever, and someday somebody would write a book about them . . .

Still, all that was rather a lot to wish for on just one Christmas, so she settled for a quiet, 'I hope it snows.'

'Imogen?' said Mrs Stewart, calling her out of her daydream. 'Shall we go downstairs for breakfast?'

Imogen's hopes for Christmas Day were certainly not disappointed.

It went, for the most part, like a normal Christmas, only none of the boring bits were boring any more.

Even when Arthur had to phone his godparents to thank them for his presents – and Arthur had never liked phone calls – he could watch Einstein getting himself tangled up in tinsel on the far side of the room, and arguing with the cat over a fish-shaped toy. Sometimes, to mix things up, Imogen would hide the toy under a cushion and watch mischievously as the two animals followed each other in circles round the sofa.

'Do you think,' said Arthur to Mrs Stewart, as Imogen distracted herself with games, 'that Theo will still want to be my friend at school?' The idea had been nagging at him ever since their trip to Edinburgh, only until now he hadn't been quite sure what it was that he was worried about.

'What do you mean, dear?' said Mrs Stewart, who was admiring the book Mr Stewart had bought her for Christmas.

'When Einstein goes home to Sydney. What if Theo doesn't like me when I don't have a penguin?'

'But Theo's only ever met Einstein once, dear,' said Mrs Stewart dismissively. 'It's not like you ever took him to school.' Then she looked suspicious.

Arthur quickly realised what he had done, and even Imogen, who had been laughing at the cat until a moment ago, turned from the sofa and looked at her brother with wide eyes.

'You didn't!' said Mrs Stewart, after a pause.

The silence answering her informed her that they did.

'I'm saying nothing,' said Mrs Stewart stiffly. She held her hands in the air and went to adjust something on the Christmas tree. 'I wish you luck if your father ever finds out!'

'Finds out what?' said Mr Stewart, who had just returned from scraping ice off the car windscreen outside.

'It wasn't me,' said Imogen quickly.

'But you *knew*!' said Arthur.

'Not at first!'

'She blackmailed me!'

'Ah,' said Mr Stewart eventually. 'Yes, I thought so. Penguins at school, hmm?'

The rest of his family looked at him in astonishment.

Mr Stewart shrugged and gave a half-smile as he hung up his coat. 'The herrings we left out were always eaten rather tidily,' he said simply. 'And Gizmo's been getting a little fat lately, don't you think?'

He wandered over to the sofa, whistled and picked up a newspaper.

'Of course Theo will still want to be your friend, Arthur,' said Imogen kindly. She was feeling a little guilty at the mention of blackmail.

'But we only made friends because of Einstein.'

'You only spoke to him because of Einstein. That's not the same thing.'

'Why don't you phone him?' suggested Mrs Stewart, who had just about recovered from her shock.

Arthur looked alarmed at the prospect.

'Go on,' said Imogen. 'You can ask him if he still wants to be friends when you wish him a happy Christmas.'

'All right . . .' said Arthur, and his stomach somersaulted as he went over to the phone.

Theo's mother picked up after a few rings.

'Merry Christmas!' Arthur mumbled, his ears going pink. 'It's Arthur. Can I speak to Theo?'

He waited for a moment while Theo came to the phone.

'Arthur!' said Theo. 'Merry Christmas!'

'Merry Christmas,' said Arthur. Then quickly, so as to get it over with: 'Einstein's going home tomorrow,' he blurted.

'Home?'

'Back to Sydney Zoo. We found Isaac, but now they want Einstein back.'

'Oh,' said Theo. 'Are you okay?'

'I think so,' said Arthur. 'Penguins aren't really meant to live in houses in London. But I hope maybe they'll let him visit.'

'Or we could go to Sydney to see him!' said Theo.

Arthur's heart lifted at that. 'So you still want to be my friend?' he said.

Theo sounded confused. 'Yes,' he said. 'Don't you?'

'Yes, of course!' said Arthur.

'Well, that's good!' said Theo. 'I need to help my

mum get dinner ready, but tell me about Isaac soon!'

'There, that wasn't so bad, was it?' said Mrs Stewart, once Arthur had put the phone down. 'Are we ready to give Einstein his Christmas presents?'

Arthur jumped up. He had been ready all day. He had painted a huge picture of Einstein and Isaac by Edinburgh Castle. Isaac's eyebrows were made of yellow pipe cleaners, his webbed feet were a string of orange fingerprints, and even Einstein's dark blue feathers were painted with a coat of glitter. It was, in everyone's opinion, his finest work to date, and the first thing to be tucked neatly into Einstein's rucksack, ready for his journey home.

Mr and Mrs Stewart had got him a framed photo of the whole family eating tea at the Balmoral Hotel. Imogen thought she looked a little silly in it, with a face full of scone, but Einstein and Isaac looked so handsome on their armchairs that she didn't really mind. And Imogen had saved him her favourite

Inspector Bucket book. She supposed that, given her success as a detective, she didn't need it so much any more, and at any rate it was something for him to remember her by. These both went in the rucksack too, along with an old scarf of Imogen's, and one of Arthur's pyjama tops. ('In case he gets cold on the flight,' Mrs Stewart explained.)

Then Imogen and Arthur opened the last of their presents, which included *more* pyjamas and *more* books, and Christmas dinner was the most delicious it had ever been, and Mr and Mrs Stewart drank rather more mulled wine than they ought to, and told Imogen off when she tried to steal some for herself.

And after more games, and Christmas crackers, and several different arguments they didn't really mean, Imogen and Arthur fell asleep in front of the telly, with the fire roaring, and Einstein snoring, and their fluffiest new Christmas socks on.

## Chapter Fourteen

# Goodbye For Now

Imogen woke up in her own bed, which was strange because she couldn't remember how she'd got there. There was a gentle tap on the door and Mrs Stewart stuck her head round it.

'Get dressed,' she said. 'It's time to take Einstein to the airport.'

Imogen's stomach sank a little. It hadn't seemed to matter so much a few days earlier because the excitement of Christmas had been enough to overpower any dread about Einstein going away.

But now Christmas was over, and it hadn't snowed – it was only raining, and to make matters worse the sun hadn't bothered to rise. She quickly dressed and hurried downstairs to the kitchen.

Her family was waiting in the hall and Einstein, for the first time in several weeks, was standing with his blue rucksack by the door. Mrs Stewart had wrapped a little scarf round his neck and given him a sandwich box of herrings, and he looked, to Imogen's disappointment, perfectly happy.

'Come on, everyone!' said Mr Stewart, in his cheery voice. 'Someone's got a plane to catch!'

As they climbed into the car, the sun was starting to think about coming up, but it wasn't yet bright enough for the streetlamps to have been switched off, and they lit up the falling raindrops one by one. Imogen stared out of the window as the car twisted through the streets away from their home and spotted several of her Missing Pengwin posters still hanging raggedly from walls and lamp posts. One of them had torn almost in half, and was blowing listlessly in the wind. She chewed the inside of her cheek and thought about how much younger and sillier she had been those two entire weeks ago. It was a long drive to Heathrow, and she drifted in and out of sleep for most of the way.

Heathrow Airport was busy, and once Mr Stewart had managed to park the car they had to weave through lots of groups of people to get to the check-in desk. Arthur kept hold of Einstein and was careful not to lose sight of his father's coat.

When they reached the desk, a friendly-looking flight attendant dressed in a uniform appeared to be waiting for them. She was holding a sign that read **Einstein** and recognised them before they recognised her – because they were, after all, the only family in Heathrow airport with a penguin.

'The Stewart family?' said the flight attendant. 'I'm here to escort an unaccompanied penguin.'

'That's us,' said Mr Stewart, and he shook her hand and started talking about something or other that was very important, like passport stamps and air turbulence.

Arthur and Imogen stayed a few metres behind him.

'I'll write to you,' said Arthur, putting Einstein down on the floor and giving him a hug. 'You can get one of the zookeepers to hand you the letters.'

'And maybe we'll visit Sydney?' said Imogen, glancing hopefully at her mother. 'And you can come back here whenever you like. Can't he, Mum?'

Departures

Mrs Stewart smiled. 'Of course,' she said. 'Penguins are always very welcome at our house. We'll just have to get the zoo's permission this time.'

'But if he's broken out once . . .' Arthur pointed out.

'Exactly,' said Imogen. 'It's only goodbye till we see him again.' She really meant it too. She knelt down and gave Einstein a big hug, and he squawked something that was probably along the lines of missing them both, and hoping they would visit Australia soon.

'Righto,' said Mr Stewart. 'Are we ready?'

'I think so,' said Arthur, and Imogen nodded.

'All right, Einstein,' said the flight attendant kindly. 'Would you like to come with me?'

The sinking feeling in Imogen's stomach was starting to disappear, turning into something that was still a little sad, but only in a temporary, happy sort of way. It was an odd way to feel, she thought, but not altogether a bad one. And so they watched Einstein walk through the airport, holding the flight attendant's hand in his flipper, until both had disappeared round the corner.

# Epilogue

Over ten thousand miles away, a disgruntled-looking detective sat forlornly on the sofa in his boss's office. His white coat was smudged with dirt, he was badly in need of a shave and his hat was nowhere to be seen.

'You're saying a penguin pecked you, and two children locked you in a store cupboard?'

The detective shivered at the word 'penguin', and spilled a small dribble of scalding-hot coffee down his shirt.

His boss looked down at him over her glasses and started to readjust the papers on her desk.

'You don't understand . . .' the detective began. 'The penguin was out of control, and the children, they weren't like ordinary children. One of them was a Detective Chief Inspector!'

'And where did you hear *that*?' asked his boss, raising a disapproving eyebrow.

He glanced round the room, as if searching his memory for something more substantial. 'Well, she told me . . .'

'I've done my own research on the case, Bill, and I can assure you that Imogen Stewart is nothing but a Year Five student with a penchant for drama. Honestly, this is worse than the time you misplaced those crocodiles in the shopping mall.'

The detective looked glum, and said nothing.

'I could understand your difficulty that time – but a penguin? Really?'

'Penguin . . .' the detective repeated under his breath. He shivered again and stared into the middle distance.

'I've been on the phone all morning, telling Sydney Zoo why a nine-year-old can solve a case my detectives can't.'

'They tied me up,' the detective whispered. 'They put a bucket on my head . . .'

'To be honest, Bill, I'm not interested,' said his boss. 'Just get out of my office.'